Can't Lose You

J.R. Brown

Cover Design by Sprinkles On Top
Studioshttp://www.sprinklesontopstudios.com

Edited by Mary Yakovets

Published by J.R. Brown

ISBN-13: 978-0692512463
ISBN-10: ISBN: 0692512462

DEDICATION

For my husband who supported me every step of the way.

J.R. BROWN

TABLE OF CONTENTS

ACKNOWLEDGMENTS

To my husband and children for being so patient and supportive of this journey every step of the way. Thank you for being a part of this with me. You have all inspired me in many ways.

To my parents for always encouraging me to always go after the things I want in life. You have always been there for me and I want to thank you both for that.

Special thanks to my family and friends that wanted to read through and give me some helpful feedback. Thank you for the love and encouragement you all showed.

To my cover designer, Sarah, from Sprinkles On Top Studios. The cover is beautiful. I appreciate everything that you did. Thank you for answering all my questions and being so patient with me.

To my editor, Mary Yakovets, thank you for all your honesty and input. You helped me to make my story a lot stronger.

Thank you to all who have been a part of this with me. I appreciate all the love and support!

CHAPTER 1

"Jayce!" I squeal as he carries me over his shoulders to my car.

"What, Elle? I need to make sure you make it safely to your car."

"I have two feet that are completely capable of walking," I giggle.

"Yeah, well, we know how clumsy you can be," Jayce says with a chuckle.

Although he does have a point, I try to act offended but fail as a laugh escapes. "I am not clumsy enough that I can't walk to my own car!" I say as I smack him on the back.

"I don't know, Elle, there was that one time..."

I smack him again to try to cut him off. I don't need to be reminded of the time where I sprained my ankle walking to my car one morning. It wasn't my fault that there was a hole in the yard that no one could see. As if reading my mind Jayce says, "And Elle, don't tell me you didn't see that hole, because then maybe you need to have your eyes checked."

"I don't need my eyes checked, Jay!" I snap. "I just wasn't paying attention. Technically it's your fault because I was reading a text from you that morning. So if anyone is to blame it is you." Real mature, I know.

"Okay, enough talk about that," Jayce says as he puts me back down on the ground by my car. He wraps his arms around my waist and presses his lips to my forehead. "Have you been thinking about some things you want to do for our last summer before we go off to college?"

Jayce and I both got accepted into Oregon State University. We have a couple more months in Portland before we make the move to Corvallis. It's not that far away, only about an hour and a half, so we will be able to come back on the weekends to visit our families. We found a duplex off campus that we are renting with two of our friends, Olivia and Evan. Olivia and I are going to rent one side and the guys are going to stay in the other. I'm so excited. This is our last summer before college and I plan to enjoy it.

I wrap my arms around his neck and look up at him. "Yep, I was thinking we could take a week trip somewhere together with Olivia and Evan," I say with a smile.

Jayce laughs, "Yeah, that'll work out well. They'll probably kill each other before the end of the trip."

It's true, they probably would. Olivia and Evan have always clashed heads with each other. I think they only put up with each other because of Jayce and me, although sometimes I wonder if they act that way toward each other because it's easier than admitting there might be something between them.

"Well, maybe some quality time will be good for them," I say with a wink and turn around to unlock my car. I begin to open my door but Jayce puts his hand out to open it for me. Before I climb in Jayce wraps his arms around me for a hug. Wrapping my arms around his waist and leaning my head on his chest, I close my eyes and listen to his heartbeat as the cool wind brushes across my face. Being cocooned like this in his arms under the stars feels so peaceful. We stand there for a few minutes before Jayce pulls my chin up with his finger. I meet his gaze as he smiles at me.

"Well, we can talk about it more tomorrow. I'll be by in the morning around nine," he says as he leans down and gives me a sweet goodnight kiss.

"Sounds good. Goodnight, Jayce," I say as I climb into my car and place the keys in the ignition. Jayce leans in and places a kiss on my nose. "Goodnight, Elle," Jayce replies as he shuts my door.

***

I get about a mile from Jayce's when I realize my gas light is still on. I forgot it came on before I got to his house earlier. I knew I should've stopped before, but I was running late meeting up with Jayce. I glance at the clock on the dash and see that it's almost one a.m., which means most gas stations are closed.

Since I was distracted with the gas light I realize that I missed my turn a ways back and will have to take the longer way back home. It also means I have to go through the not-so-good side of town. As I continue driving I see a gas station up ahead.

Go figure the only gas station that is open this late is a rundown place that doesn't even look like they are open. The flashing red "Open" signs begs to differ. I pull up to the pump and turn my car off, get out and take a look around. I notice most of the street lights are burned out, and only one light shines on the gas station parking lot.

"Great," I mutter as I unscrew the cap and put in the pump. After pushing a few buttons I stand and wait. A shiver runs down my spine as I take in the rest of my surroundings. The shops across the streets are definitely closed or abandoned. I think one of them even has a broken window or two. I glance in the gas station window and don't see anyone inside.

"This keeps getting better and better." I begin to take the pump out when my phone alerts me of a text. I finish putting the pump away and screw on the gas cap. Pulling out my phone I see a text from Jayce.

Jayce: *Did you make it home yet?*

Me: *No, I had to stop and get gas. I'll be home soon though.*

Jayce: *Ok, be safe.*

Jayce: *Sleep in love, Sleep in peace,*
My love for you will never cease.

Me: *Like a puzzle with one piece,*
My heart to you I now release.

With a smile on my face I shove my phone back in my pocket and grab my purse. I walk the short distance to the door and go inside. I look around but don't see any employees. I approach the counter hoping someone will notice so I can get out of this rundown place. After standing there a few moments with no response I lean over the counter to get a better look in the back room. I don't see anyone. "Excuse me!" I call as I continue to look around. Still no response.

I start to turn when I hear a loud crash come from the back room. Startled by the noise, I whirl back around and that's when I begin to hear yelling from the back room.

"Excuse me!" I yell as I try to lean farther over the counter. Still nothing. I know it's probably not okay to go behind the counter, but I'm so ready to be out of this place and heading home that I go around the counter to head toward the back room. I see a door partially open down the short hallway. As I approach I see that there are papers, a broken vase, and the desk flipped over on the floor, which is probably what caused the loud noise. I move with my back pressed to the wall as I quietly creep toward the room. Peeking through the crack of the door I see two men facing each other, and from the looks of it they aren't happy with one another.

Compared to my five foot one height these men are huge. Both men are easily over six foot; although one is a few inches shorter they are both built like tanks. I decide that this is probably not a situation I want to be in, so I begin to turn to go back when I'm stopped dead in my tracks...

"Where is the money?" Tank One yells as he slams Tank Two into the wall.

"Tony, I j-just need a l-little more t-time," Tank Two gasps out.

"The boss has given you an extra week and has lost his patience with you!"

"I-I don't have it right now, but I..."

"Boss said you would say that, so he sent me to take care of it!" Tank One, who I now know is Tony, interrupts.

BANG! BANG!

I gasp as I watch Tank Two fall to the ground and my hands fly over my mouth. The floor around him begins to turn red as blood spills out. My body begins to tremble as I walk slowly backwards and it becomes hard to breathe. Tony must've heard me because now he is looking right at me with a scowl on his face. I turn to run but he grabs my wrist. I try to pull free but his grip on my hand tightens and I whimper as I feel my bones being crushed together.

"P-please let me go! I-I won't say anything. I was just trying to get gas so I could get home. P-please, let me go!" I cry. I begin to feel tears run down my face. My body is shaking so bad that I don't know if I'll be able to make it out.

"You aren't going anywhere," he says as he shoves me into the wall. My head slams against the wall and it becomes hard to see. I try to calm myself down enough so that I can think of a way out of this. I glance around the small hallway and find nothing that will be helpful. Then I remember the pepper spray in my purse.

"I really need to go h-home. People will be looking for me. I j-just want to go home!" I cry as I slowly reach one hand down into my purse. If I can just distract him long enough to grab it...He holds me against the wall and lowers his face in front of mine. "Like I said, you aren't going anywhere. You are going to come with me and the boss can figure out what to do with you."

It's then that I notice a jagged scar running from his left eye down to his lower jaw. My eyes flicker from his scar back to his eyes. His eyes are a dull gray and you can see the anger, hate, and loneliness in them. I continue to study his features and continue up to his hair, which is a deep brown, almost black. My fingers wrap tightly around the pepper spray as I slowly inch it out of my purse.

My eyes glance back to his scar as I quietly ask, "Where did you get the scar from?"

He stares at me for what seems like a long time. I begin to wonder if he's going to answer, which I don't really care if he does. I just need him to get distracted. A slow evil grin begins to spread across his face. "That's what could happen to you if you don't listen...or worse."

I quickly pull the pepper spray up and spray him directly in the eyes. I'm instantly released as he stumbles away, yelling and rubbing at his face. Running as fast as I can I head straight for my car. Thankfully my keys are still in the ignition and I start my car and peel out of the gas station. I go to grab my phone to call 911 but I'm shaking so badly I end up dropping it. I decide to leave it and drive straight to the police station as fast as I can.

Five minutes later I pull into the station. I race from the car straight to the building. Once inside I bend over, trying to catch my breath. I must've startled the lady behind the desk because she stands up from her chair and walks over to the window. "Can I help you, ma'am?"

It's then that the adrenaline drains and I crumble to the floor crying and trying to catch my breath as I say, "There was a-a man, and h-he s-shot another m-m-man!" From that point on the rest of the night becomes a blur...

**

After I calmed down enough the police began their questions. I explained everything that I remembered from how I got there to what the men looked like and everything between. They showed me pictures and asked if I recognized either of the men from the photos. Thankfully I paid attention to the guy Tony's features because it turns out he works for a big mob in Portland. The police and FBI have been working on a case involving this mob for several years now and haven't had enough evidence to put them behind bars. Sometime during my questioning my parents were called and arrived just as the police finished their interview.

"Elizabeth! Oh honey, are you okay?" My mom rushes over to me and pulls me into a hug. I hug her back like she is my lifeline and begin to cry again.

"Shhh, it's okay, sweetie. You're safe now. You're going to be okay. We have you now," my mom whispers as she rubs my back. My dad comes over and joins in on our hug and comforts me too. We all turn as we hear an officer come in and clear his throat.

"Miss Elizabeth, there are a couple more things we need to tell you, so if you and your parents could please sit," the officer says as he gestures to the chairs in front of him. We release each other and take the seats he indicated.

"Elizabeth, with the things that you witnessed tonight we have enough evidence now to at least bring in the suspect that shot the guy at the gas station. If we can bring him in we are hoping to be able to get more information out of him, and hopefully be able to shut down this mob."

"That's good, right?" I ask.

"Yes, well, I'm not done. In order to bring him in and keep him we need you to testify."

"O-okay..."

"Isn't there another way that you can bring him in without having to involve our daughter? Don't you think she has been through enough as it is?" my mom interrupts.

The officer looks over at my parents. "I'm sorry, but no, there isn't. I understand your concern, ma'am. I have children of my own and wouldn't want them to have to go through this, but it will help get these bad men off the streets. Now, there is more." He clears his throat and continues. "When your daughter ran out of the gas station she left her purse there, which contained her driver's license and other things that can be used for information about her. So we recommend that your family go into the Witness Protection Program." He looks over to me as he finishes.

I sit there stunned as the officer continues on with information about the program. I've heard of witness protection in movies, TV, and books but I never thought I would have to be a part of that. I won't be Elizabeth Grace Payton who just graduated high school anymore. I won't get to see my house that we have lived in for the last six years. I won't get to see my friends anymore. I won't get to move into our duplex with Olivia.

And then it hits me hard as I realize... "I'll never get to see Jayce again," I whisper as I begin to cry. He was supposed to pick me up in the morning and we were going to spend the day together with Olivia and Evan. We were all supposed to spend our last summer together before we go to college, the college we were going to go to together! Jayce and I even talked about getting married someday when we graduate. Yes, some people say we are too young, but it has always felt right for us. My heart begins to break as it all begins to sink in. Millions of things I will never get to do with the people I love. People I will never be able to see or contact again. This can't be happening! It can't be; maybe I will wake up and this will all be just a nightmare!

I come back to what the officer is saying as he places folders in front of me and my parents. I grab my folder and slowly open it, and there it is in bold print.

Riley Lynn Anderson

I am now Riley Lynn Anderson and we are being moved to Virginia Beach, Virginia.

CHAPTER 2

Almost three years later

Today is my first day at a new school, and of course it's a month into the school year already. So not only am I the new student, but I am the new student starting late. We just moved to Portland from Seattle. My dad got transferred here for his job. This is the worst time he could've gotten transferred. I had just started eighth grade back home in Seattle and two weeks into the school year, my dad gets informed that he is being transferred here.

As I'm walking down the hall of the middle school, I'm trying to look at the map to make sure I get to the right class. The halls are pretty empty, so I'm not really paying attention to where I'm going. I go to turn down a hall when I slam into something. My books and papers drop to the floor and scatter.

"I'm sorry! Are you okay?"

I look up and realize I didn't run into something, but someone. He is a really cute someone, if I'm being honest. His hair is a deep chocolate and long enough to just barely touch his eyes. My eyes find his and I notice his eyes are even darker than his hair, but still the chocolate color. It's then that I realize that I have been staring and don't even remember what he asked. He must read my mind because a smile spreads across his face. "I'm sorry, are you okay?" I nod, because apparently I can't get a word out, and begin to pick up my books and papers.

"Here, let me help you."

"Thanks," I say as he hands me the rest of my things.

"Are you new? I've never seen you around."

"Yeah, we just moved here," I smile shyly.

"What class are you going to? I can show you if you want," he offers as he glances down at my schedule. I point to the class, and he nods. "That's actually the same class I'm going to." He begins walking and I fall into step with him.

I take quick glances his way and can't help but smile. He is really cute. I've never really noticed boys much, but I can't help but notice this one. He looks over and smirks. "I'm Jayce, by the way. Jayce Cooper." He continues to stare at me, and then I realize I never told him my name.

"Oh um, Elizabeth. Elizabeth Payton." Smooth, Elizabeth, real smooth.

"Well, Elizabeth, if you want I can continue to show you around to your classes today."

"That would be great. Thanks." A big smile spreads across my face and he returns it. It's then I begin to think that maybe moving here wasn't such a bad thing. Just as we get to our class the bell begins to ring....

I open my eyes, trying to clear the fog and wonder why the bell is still ringing. I look over and realize it's my alarm. Turning over, I shut my alarm off and flop back down on my back. That's the third dream in the past two weeks that has been about times with Jayce. The dreams come in phases, and they are always memories of my life before. My eyes begin to water as I think of the day I met Jayce.

After that day Jayce welcomed me into his group of friends. That's how I met Olivia and we instantly clicked. We became best friends. As the years went on Olivia, Evan, Jayce, and I all became close and we did almost everything together. Although Olivia and Evan always had something to fight over, we all still had a blast together. Jayce told me one time that Olivia and Evan didn't always fight like that, but neither one would ever explain what happened.

I'm startled out of my memories as a pillow hits me in the face. "Hey, what was that for?" I ask as I move the pillow off my face.

"That is for you not turning your alarm off for the last ten minutes! Now get up, Riles, we have class to get to!"

I sit up as Daphne, my roommate, walks out of my room. Things are getting better now that some time has passed. After we left the police station that night my parents and I were sent to a hotel where we stayed for a week or so. Once our "safe house" was ready here in Virginia Beach we were packed up in a private jet and flown out here.

The first three months I was like a walking zombie. I could hardly sleep because when I closed my eyes the nightmares began. The dreams would take me back to the night at the gas station and watching the murder. Sometimes it would play out differently though and include Jayce and my friends. I would always end up taken away from them, just like I am now. Most nights I would wake up screaming and crying.

I spent a lot of my time in bed just lying there. I would hardly eat anything because I didn't have much of an appetite. I pretty much just started wasting away. I lost weight; my body was already small, so I became pretty skinny. My parents really struggled to get me to do anything. They didn't know what to do for me. Looking back I know things weren't easy for them either; I mean, they had to leave their life too and adjust to a new one. I felt a lot of guilt, and still do sometimes now, like this is my fault. If I wouldn't have stopped at that gas station that night we could still be in Portland. I could be going to college at Oregon State working toward my veterinary medicine degree and spending my college years with Jayce and our friends.

After the first few months I slowly started doing more things and beginning my new life. I never went out to do anything with anyone but my parents. I didn't try to make any friends and mostly kept to myself. I never knew if we would be relocated so I didn't see a point in making friends. My parents tried to encourage me to go out and meet people. But I didn't want new friends; I wanted my friends back from Portland. I wanted my old life back.

My parents finally talked me into going to talk to someone. I saw a counselor regularly for a while. She talked me into finding something that would help me, so I started taking kickboxing classes to help me work through my issues. It really began to make a difference and eventually the nightmares began to come less often, I got my appetite back, and started gaining some weight.

After seven months my parents and counselor talked me into getting a job. They told me it would be good for me to get out of the house more and begin living. I began applying for jobs and took a position as a receptionist at a physical therapy clinic. I have worked there ever since.

It took about eleven months for the police and FBI to wrap up the case and trial for the mob back in Portland. They were able to get everyone in the mob convicted and locked up except for the boss, who I found out is named Frank. They haven't been able to find him, so even today we still need to be careful. We have been warned that he may come after me since I was the key witness that shut his organization down, but so far they haven't found him.

"Riles! Get up and get in the shower or you're going to be late for class. We have thirty minutes!" Daphne yells from the hall, bringing me back to reality.

"Yeah, yeah. I'm getting up now! Calm your horses!" I say as I roll out of bed.

I walk over to my closet, grab some clothes, and head for the shower. After I shower and dress I begin fixing my hair. When we came to Virginia Beach I dyed my hair a red auburn color. I wanted something different that wouldn't remind me of before. My hair is a natural honey color, and I used to keep it shoulder-length with bangs in the front. Now my hair is grown down to the middle of my back and I grew my bangs out. I actually love my new hair color and length.

Instead of drying my hair I decide to use some mousse and leave it curly. After I fix my hair I put on some black eye liner and mascara and call it good. I rush out the bathroom to my room, grab my things and head out to the kitchen.

As I get to the kitchen I notice Daphne sitting at the table with a cup of coffee in hand and another sitting across from her. I walk over and sit down. "Thanks. I really needed this today," I say as I look up at her.

"No problem." She glances up. "So do you work this afternoon?"

"Yeah. I just have the one class this morning and then work one to six."

"Awesome, because I was thinking we could go out tonight. I want to start Spring Break early! I need a night out." Daphne says as she gets up to put her cup in the sink.

"I don't know, Daph, I have a few assignments to

finish up before break starts next week," I say as I go to put my cup in the sink and grab my books, keys, and phone off the counter.

Daphne turns to face me. "Oh, come on! Those assignments aren't due till after break. Plus, you haven't been out since your birthday three weeks ago. That is not normal for people that are in college. You're twenty-one now, which means we can go drink legally, and we don't have to sneak you in," she says with a wink.

She is right, I haven't been out since then. We went out dancing for my birthday. We met up with a few people from our classes and people continuously bought me drinks throughout the night. I ended up with the worst hangover the next day. I spent the day and most of the evening in bed or in the bathroom. After that I haven't really made time to go out, and instead stayed focused on work and school.

I roll my eyes. "Yeah, I know I have been doing what a college student should be doing." I pause and look up at her and put on a sweet smile. "Keeping up with my schoolwork."

Now it's Daphne who rolls her eyes. "Yeah, whatever. You're coming anyways. I will drag you out of here if I have to so be ready to go by eight," she calls over her shoulder as she walks out the door.

"Great," I mutter as I walk out the door behind her and lock it. We take the stairs down to the lobby. As we walk out we wave and say hi to Phil, the security man for our apartment building. Phil glances up from the computer and waves, then goes back to looking at the screen. Phil is an older man probably in his sixties. At first glance he looks like an old grumpy man, but he's really a sweet guy once you get to know him.

When we get outside Daphne and I go our separate ways to our cars.

"See you later!" I call over to Daphne.

"You bet! Don't forget—eight o'clock—be ready to party!" she calls back as she climbs in her car and shuts the door. I smile and roll my eyes as I get into my car. I look at the clock on the dash and realize I have just enough time to get to class without being late.

Working as a receptionist for a physical therapy clinic was actually what made me decide to start going to college. When we first moved here I didn't see a point in going because I had no motivation to do anything. My dreams of becoming a veterinarian didn't sound as exciting anymore, and nothing else sounded any better. After working a few months at the clinic I began learning more about physical therapy and became more interested in it. One of the girls I work with told me about South University's physical therapy assistant two year degree program. So that summer I got enrolled for the fall semester.

Once I got accepted our marshal found an apartment right off campus that has good security for me to move into. Before then I had been living with my parents in the house that we were placed into when we first got here. After I got settled the marshal told me that I would have a roommate, which is where Daphne comes in.

Daphne came into my life at a time that I really needed a good friend. I was finally beginning to get my life on track again, and becoming friends with her was another step in the right direction. Daphne is finishing her third year at South University, working toward her bachelors in nursing. So she has another year to go. I'm finishing up my second year, so I'll be graduating at the end of this semester. I'm definitely looking forward to being done.

I pull into the parking lot, grab my things, and head to class. I get to my seat just as the professor comes into the room. I like that the classes are small, but if you're late then they usually notice. I pull out my notebook and pen and prepare to take notes. Thankfully class goes by quick, and before I know it I'm walking out the door toward my car.

"Riley! Wait up!" I hear someone yell as I approach the parking lot. I turn, look over my shoulder and see Gavin running to catch up.

"Hey Gavin," I say as I turn around. I met Gavin in one of my classes last semester. We became friends and studied together, and eventually we tried going out.

While we were dating I would constantly compare him to Jayce. Gavin is six foot and has a lean muscular body. He has shorter blond hair and bright blue eyes. He is definitely hot and a very sweet guy, but he's not Jayce. It's been almost three years and I still can't get over him. Gavin was understanding when I explained that I thought I was over an old boyfriend but realized I'm not. Which I didn't think I was but I was kind of hoping that I would get there once I started dating, but I didn't tell him that. After that we decided to just be friends, and it has been great ever since.

Gavin stops in front of me. "So I heard Daph is dragging you out tonight," he says with a smirk. I turn to the car and shove my stuff in the backseat, then face him.

"Yeah, and I really don't want to go. But I'll give in to her little plan since it has been awhile, although I'm sure she'll be dragging me to go out every night during Spring Break next week. Are you coming out with us tonight?" I ask.

"Yeah, you know Daph. If she goes out then she wants everyone to go out," he replies with a chuckle. "Matt was going to come but he isn't going make it." Matt is one of Gavin's friends that goes out with us sometimes. "I think a few of the other guys are going to meet up with us later though."

"Cool."

"Well, I'll see ya tonight then. I need to get to my next class," Gavin says as he begins to walk backwards toward the building.

"Yep, see you tonight," I answer then turn to get in my car and drive to work.

CHAPTER 3

"Oh good, you're home!"

"Ah yes, nothing like being welcomed home after such a long day of work," I laugh as I walk through the door. I go back to my room and put my things away. When I come back out Daphne says, "I figured you hadn't eaten dinner yet so I ordered take-out. It should be here any time."

"You're awesome! Thanks, I'm starving," I say as I sit at the table. "So I heard Gavin is coming with us tonight."

"Yeah, I ran into him this morning." She comes to sit across from me. "Plus, you never know—maybe you guys will get back together," she smiles with a wink.

I roll my eyes. "Daph, we already talked about this. Gavin and I have tried. Yes, he is a great guy, but I'm just not ready for a relationship. Plus, Gavin and I are great friends, and we both agree it's better this way."

"I know, I know. I just like giving you a hard time. So are you ever going to tell me the details about the boy who still has your heart?" she asks as she gives me the puppy eyes.

Over the past year and a half Daphne and I have become close, but of course there are things I can't tell her. I told her that my parents and I moved here from Iowa. We don't have any other relatives, which is true. Both my parents don't have any siblings, and both sets of grandparents died when I was young. I told her my dad got transferred here, and I wanted to move somewhere warm and on the coast so I moved with them. I also told her the reason I took the year off from school was because I wasn't sure what I wanted to go for, which at the time was true. I have never given her much information about Jayce. She knows there is a boy that I was with for a couple years and that things didn't end well, and I have never gotten over him fully.

"Nope, that topic is a sensitive one that I'm not ready to talk about and don't know when I will be." I smile as our food arrives, which thankfully means this conversation is over. I'm sure she would've stopped asking anyways. Daphne and I are the same in that we are both very private people, which I pretty much have to be now. Even before I was always kind of a quiet person. I think that's why Daphne and I get along so well because we understand each other and know when not to push.

I get up, get the plates and we begin to dish out our food. As we eat we stay to lighter conversation, talking about school, and I tell her about work. After we are done eating we clean up the mess, then we go to our rooms to get ready.

I go to my closet and pick out a pair of dark boot cut jeans and a fitted white short-sleeve top with a design on it, then head for the bathroom to change and get ready. I decide to leave my hair curly, then touch up my eyeliner and mascara. I walk back out to my room to get my clutch, keys, phone, and black boots, then head out to the family room.

As I'm putting my last boot on Daphne comes out. Daphne is five foot five and has a thin hourglass figure. Tonight she has her golden blonde hair left straight, her makeup lightly done that still makes her light brown eyes stand out, and is wearing a pair of dark skinny jeans with a cute powder blue top.

"So you ready to go? Gavin said he would come pick us up so we don't have to drive." she says as she gets up to get her clutch off the counter.

"Yeah, I actually am looking forward to going. I think you're right—I needed to get out tonight. Plus, I don't have class tomorrow so I'll get to sleep in."

"I thought you had one tomorrow. They cancel it?"

"Yep, the professor emailed me while I was getting ready, so looks like my Spring Break starts tonight." I look over and smile.

"I wish my teachers would cancel my classes tomorrow. I have tests in both classes and I have to get up at eight."

I look down at my phone as I receive a text. "Time to go, Gavin is here."

Once we get to the lobby we see Gavin waiting by the door. He smiles and walks over. "Don't you ladies look beautiful as always." He holds out both arms to us.

"Thank you, you don't look too bad yourself," I say as I link my arm through his and smile up at him. Daphne hooks her arm through his other arm as she says thanks. We make our way out to Gavin's truck and he opens the passenger side door for us to get in. Daphne climbs in back and I climb in front. Once he's in we drive to the club.

***

We arrive at the club a little after eight-thirty and it is already busy for a Thursday night. As we walk through the doors I begin to feel the music pulse throughout my body. Gavin weaves us through the crowd and finds us a table in the back. Once we are seated he heads to the bar to get us all drinks. I glance around and recognize a few people from my classes. Daphne pulls her chair up next to me and sits down. She looks around, then leans over toward me. "Looks like other people had the same idea we had. It is never this busy on a Thursday, especially this early."

I nod and glance around. A few minutes later I look toward the bar and see Gavin heading our way with the drinks. Several girls try to get his attention as he weaves his way back to our table. He smiles and nods at them but continues his way toward us. When he gets to the table he sets two beers and a fruity mixed drink down. "One beer for you, Daph," he says as he sets a beer in front of Daphne. "And one girly drink for you, Riley," he says as he places mine in front of me.

"Then the drink is very fitting for me," I laugh. He chuckles and begins drinking his beer. Daphne and I say thanks and sip our drinks. The next couple hours we visit, dance, and down a couple more beverages. I just finished my third when Daphne comes up and grabs my arm. "Come on, let's go dance. I love this song!" I set my glass down and we wave to Gavin as we head toward the dance floor. He waves and goes back to visiting with a guy from his class.

I laugh as I stumble while Daphne pulls me through the crowd to the dance floor. Once we get to the middle Daphne stops and we begin moving our hips to the beat of the song. As we're dancing I begin to glance around the club, not really looking for anyone particular.

I see a few girls from my class dancing not far from us. There are a lot of people seated up at the bar waiting for drinks. All the tables in the club are filled with people. I notice small groups standing around visiting. Daphne was right, this place is really busy for a Thursday night.

I turn my gaze back over to the bar and feel time stop. My breath gets caught in my throat. My heart rate picks up and feels like it's going to beat out of my chest. This isn't possible. There's no way that's who I think it is. He lives on the other side of the country. What would the chances be that he would be here in Virginia Beach, in this club, the same night as me? The odds don't even seem possible. They shouldn't be possible. But he is, and I know it's him. I would know him anywhere. He's filled out more over the last few years, but still lean and muscular, maybe even taller. His hair is shorter now, but still the same dark chocolate, and the same sweet smile.

"Jayce..." I gasp. I feel tears begin to prick my eyes. My heart is telling me to go up to him and tell him I'm sorry for leaving him, tell him how much I love him, and that I never got over him. I shake my head. As much as it hurts I can't do that. He can't know I'm here because that could put all of us at risk.

"Riles!"

All of a sudden Daphne is in my face grabbing my arms, "Riley! Look at me!" I look at her and see her searching my face with a confused expression. "Are you okay? You look like you've seen a ghost."

I nod, "Yeah, um..." I wipe under my eyes and shake my head to clear my mind. "I'm ready to go home. I need to go home," I say as I glance over her shoulder. I look where I saw Jayce by the bar but he's gone. Maybe I was just seeing things; either way I need to get out of here.

Daphne nods and begins pulling me toward our table. When we reach it Daphne says something to

Gavin. I'm still in a daze so I don't hear what is being said. Next thing I know Gavin is leading us out of the club and putting me in the front seat of his truck.

Before he shuts the door he scans my face with concern. "Riles, are you okay? You don't look so good." My hands begin to twist in my lap. I look down at my hands as my eyes begin to prick with tears. With his hand Gavin brings my chin up to look at him. "Hey, what's going on? Did something happen?" He looks back at Daphne. "Did something happen to her while you guys were dancing?"

"I don't know what happened. We were dancing, laughing and having a good time. Then all of a sudden she stopped dancing and her face turned white like she had seen a ghost or something. It took a few tries to get her to respond to me," Daphne says with an edge of panic in her voice.

Gavin nods and looks back at me. "Riles, we're going to get you home, okay? You're going to be okay."

I nod and he shuts the door and walks around to his side.

The drive home is quiet, which I'm sure is because no one knows what to say. I don't even know what to say. I have about a million questions running through my head. Why is Jayce in Virginia Beach? Who came with him? Did he somehow find out where I went? Is he still living in Oregon? Does he have a girlfriend?

I know we aren't together but that last question hurts to think about. I know I shouldn't expect him to not be with anyone. I don't even know what he thinks happened to me. My parents never told me what people were going to think happened to us, and I didn't ask because it would hurt even more knowing. I couldn't even imagine Jayce believing that I would hurt him that much and just leave when we had plans the next day and pretty much the next four years of our life, maybe more.

I thought things were beginning to get better and I felt like I was starting to move on in my life somewhat. Okay, maybe not really, but I could try to convince myself. Tonight just proved that I'm definitely not over him. I wanted to run up and hug him, kiss him, and tell him I still love him. But he can't know I'm here, and it took everything in me to not to throw my arms around him.

"Riles, we're here," Gavin says quietly, breaking me from my thoughts. I glance out the window at my apartment as Gavin comes around and opens our door. He helps Daphne down and whispers something to her. She gives me a hug. "I don't know what happened but I'm sure everything will be okay. I'm here if you need me," she whispers, then turns to head up to our place. Gavin places his hands on the sides of my face and brings it up to look at him.

"Hey," he whispers as he brushes tears I didn't realize were falling off my cheek. "Did someone hurt you tonight?" I shake my head and begin to sob. Gavin wraps his arms around me and pulls me into a hug. "Do you want to talk about it?" I shake my head again as I begin to cry harder. I wrap my arms around him and grip the back of his shirt. Gavin holds me and comforts me as I fall apart.

I don't know how long we stay there like that, but eventually he carries me up to my room. He walks over to my bed and lays me down, then he pulls the covers back and tucks me in. I feel like a little child but I'm too heartbroken to care.

"Goodnight, Riles, I'll see you in the morning," he says quietly and shuts the door as he walks out.

CHAPTER 4

The next morning I wake up to pans being slammed around in the kitchen which does not help the pounding of my head. I know I didn't drink enough to give me a headache this morning so why does it hurt so bad? Then it hits me. We went out to the club, we were dancing and having a good time. Things were going great, and then I saw Jayce and freaked out. I grab a pillow and pull it over my face. Great, my friends got to witness what a basket case I am. I'm sure they have about a million questions, but that makes three of us. I toss my pillow across the room and roll over.

"Oomph. Well, good morning to you too, Miss Sunshine."

I turn toward the door and see Daphne leaning against the door frame smiling while holding the pillow I just tossed.

"I don't know about the good part. My head is pounding."

Daphne walks over and sits on the edge of my bed. She watches me a moment. "Do you want to talk about last night?" she asks quietly as she looks at me with concern. Which I don't blame her; I acted like a crazy person.

"Which part? The part where you got to witness what a basket case your roommate is?" I ask, trying make light of the situation.

She puts her hand on my arm. "Hey, I don't think you're a basket case. I know something big must've happened though for you to get upset like that."

"I don't know if I want to talk about it," I whisper and turn away. My eyes start to water just thinking about it.

"Okay, I won't push. You can trust me, you know? I'm here if you change your mind. I made you some breakfast so come out when you're ready," she says as she gets up and walks toward my door.

"I saw him!" I blurt out just as she reaches the threshold. She turns around and studies me for a moment.

I sit up in my bed and rest against the headboard. "I saw him," I say again quieter and look down at my lap. I know I can't tell her everything, but I trust her enough to know who I'm talking about.

Daphne walks back over and sits on the edge of my bed next to me. "Who?" she asks just as quietly, almost as if she is afraid I'll shut down.

"The boy...well, I guess man now, but the one who I never got over. I saw him last night at the club. He looks a little different, shorter hair and filled out more, but I would recognize him anywhere. It was him, I know it was."

"Wow, um, yeah...that's not what I expected," she says, shocked. "Does he know you live here?"

"No...I mean, I don't think so. I never told him." I take a deep breath and begin with the story since I know she wants to ask the questions anyway. "We met when we were thirteen. I had just started a new school and ran into him...literally." I smile as I remember that day. "He helped me pick up my books and ended up having the same class as me, so he walked with me to class. He introduced me to his two best friends and from that day on we all became best friends. When we were in tenth grade he asked me to Homecoming, and the night of the dance he asked me to be his girlfriend. We were together most of high school after that. We did break up for a short time, but eventually we got back together." I close my eyes as the tears begin to run down my cheeks. "I haven't talked to him since we moved here," I whisper. I reach my hands up and wipe the tears off while Daphne sits there and doesn't say anything. I'm sure she is wondering why we would move if I had a boyfriend that I was obviously in love with, but I can't tell her.

Several minutes pass with still nothing said. I don't blame her though; there's no right thing to say to all that. I'm sure she has more questions, but she knows I'm a private person and I'll tell her things in my own time. Daphne scoots over and pulls me into a hug. She rubs my back as I begin to cry again. Once I calm down I move back and wipe the tears away.

"Please don't say anything to anyone. I don't even know what to tell Gavin. He probably thinks I'm a nutcase too."

"I won't. As far as Gavin I don't think he thinks that about you. He does care about you though. He was really worried about you last night. He said he was coming by this morning." She glances over at my clock. "Actually he should be here any time." She begins to get up off the bed and head for the door.

"Hey Daph." She stops and turns. "Why do you think he was here?" I don't expect her to know the answer but I have to ask to get it out. It's the question I've been asking over and over since I saw him.

She looks down then looks back up at me, and a slow smile spreads across her face, "I don't know, Riles, but maybe this is your sign that you'll get a second chance with him or some closure." With that said she turns and exits my room.

I sit there and think about what she said. I can't have a second chance or do closure. My closure was me moving across the country with a new identity so I could be safe. It's not safe for him to know that I'm here because Frank the mob boss is still out there somewhere looking for me. Sure, I have a different name and it would definitely be a lot harder to find me, but not impossible. Plus, I don't even know if I'll see Jayce again. With that last thought I roll out of bed and decide to just let it go because chances are I won't see him again.

I walk over to my closet, get a change of clothes, and go take a shower. Afterward I get dressed, throw my hair up into a messy bun, and head to the kitchen. As I'm walking over to the table to sit down I remember something. "Daph, didn't you have class this morning?"

She glances up at me, then continues fixing our plates. She brings the food over and sets them down before she responds. "Yeah, but I wanted to be here for you this morning and make sure you were okay." She sits down across from me and smiles. "Plus, I didn't study very much for one of the tests so I emailed my teachers saying I wouldn't be in class. They replied back and told me I can make them up after break."

"Thanks, Daph. I feel bad that I made you miss your classes though."

She waves me off. "Don't worry about it."

We eat in silence and just as we are finished there's a knock on the door and Gavin walks in.

"Hey." He walks over to the table and sits down

between Daphne and me. We both look up and smile in greeting. Daphne gets up, picks up our plates and takes them over to the sink to rinse them off. She comes back and sets a plate down in front of Gavin. He looks up. "Thanks, you know me too well." He chuckles and begins eating. Daphne walks back over to the sink and begins washing the dishes and cleaning up the mess.

Halfway through eating Gavin looks up at me and I already know what's coming, so before he can ask I respond first. "I'm sorry if I freaked you out last night and I'm sure you want an explanation...,"

Gavin puts his hand on my arm and stops me. "Hey, you don't have to explain if you don't want to. Yes, it freaked me out, but I just want to know if you're okay now. If you want to tell me I'm here to listen, but if you don't want to then I accept that too." I look up and see the sincere look in his eyes.

I nod. "Thank you. I'm better now—let's just say I ran into a surprise last night that I never expected. But things are fine now. I'll be okay." I look up at him and smile. "Thank you for bringing me home and being there during my freak out moment," I say sincerely. "Definitely not one of my finest moments, that's for sure," I add, trying to lighten the mood.

He chuckles. "You're welcome. Hey, it's okay— sometimes we all need a freak out moment," he replies with a wink. Conversation becomes lighter and Daphne comes over and joins us. After a while Gavin leaves, saying he had things to get done before he takes off for his trip and would text me later. He's going to Vegas with some of his friends for break.

After he leaves I call my parents and decide to go have lunch and spend the day with them. Once I get off the phone I go into my room to get my things.

I keep going back and forth about whether I should tell my parents that I saw Jayce. Part of me wants to tell them, but they will probably tell me if I see him again to avoid him and try not to be seen. If I did see him again I don't think I would be able to ignore him this time because I want to talk to him. There is so much that was left unsaid. I decide for now I won't say anything to my parents.

I walk into the family room and see Daphne sitting on the couch watching some TV. I sit down by her. "Hey, thanks again for breakfast and, well, everything else that you've helped me with in the last twenty-four hours," I say with a laugh. "I was thinking tonight on my way home I'll swing by and pick up a pizza and ice cream. We can pig out and maybe watch some chick flicks."

"Is this your way of paying me back?" She nudges me in the arm. "Actually, that sounds great. I don't have anything planned."

I get up and slip my shoes on. "All right...well, I'm going to my parents' but I will see you tonight."

CHAPTER 5

The next morning I walk into the kitchen and make myself a bowl of cereal. I finish pouring myself a glass of milk and go to put it away when Daphne comes in. "I'll need that so you can leave it out." I set the milk back on the counter, grab my breakfast and walk over to the table. I begin eating as Daphne gets her breakfast and comes over and sits across from me. We both eat in silence, neither of us being a morning person, even if we got to sleep in a little later.

"So I was thinking about going to the beach today after lunch since it's supposed to get up to the high seventies. Figure better enjoy these random warm days while we can. You want to come?" I ask as I go over and rinse my dishes out.

"Yeah, that sounds good." She finishes up her breakfast and goes to rinse out her dishes. Once we clean up the kitchen we spend the rest of the morning cleaning up the apartment. Between the two of us it takes about an hour. Once I'm done cleaning I fix us a quick lunch of sandwiches and chips.

Daphne offers to clean up the mess so I go in to

my room to get changed. In my closet I grab my simple black and white bikini, a pair of jean shorts, and a light green zip up jacket. A quick trip to the bathroom to change into my clothes, throw my hair up into a ponytail and I call it good. As I walk out of the bathroom I gather up towels and lotion and toss them in my bag. I glance around the room to see if I got everything before walking out to the kitchen.

A few minutes later Daphne comes out and we leave for the beach. Once we're in the car we roll the windows down and begin singing along with some country music. Fifteen minutes later we are pulling into the parking lot. After grabbing our stuff I put my sunglasses on and glance around the shore.

The beach is busy. There's volleyball nets up with games going on. Parents watching their kids play in the sand. Groups of teenagers and people our age gathered around listening to music and visiting. People laying out. I look out toward the ocean and notice a few crazy people out in the water. Yes, I call them crazy because there is no way the water is warm. Daphne follows my gaze and shakes her head. "Can you believe someone is crazy enough to get in the water? We've had, like, maybe ten days where it has been above seventy this month."

I shake my head and laugh. "There always has to be someone crazy enough to do it."

We begin walking toward the sand and look around for a spot to settle. We decide on a place and begin laying our towels down. It's warmed up enough that I decide to take off my zip up and shorts. After applying my lotion I kick my sandals off and lay back on my towel. A moment later Daphne does the same next to me.

We lay there in silence and I'm thankful for it. A light ocean breeze blows across my body and I close my eyes. Listening to the ocean waves crash on the shore, I begin to relax. I love coming to the beach, listening to the waves and feeling the wind blow across my face. As I lay there I can hear laughter from people around us. Off to my left I hear a little girl giggling as she is being chased by her mom. I look over and smile as I watch them.

I hope to have a family someday. I always wanted a large family. Growing up it was always just me and my parents. I didn't have cousins because my parents were both only children. I had grandparents and was told I saw them often when they were alive. I was so young when they passed that I don't really remember them. My parents had friends with kids so I was able to be around other children growing up, but it's just not the same as family.

"Jay, wanna go play a game of volleyball?" I'm startled out of my thinking and begin looking around for who said that.

I then see a tall blond-haired guy run over to what I'm assuming is his friend. "Yeah, wait up!"

I watch as they walk away. Maybe I am going crazy. I hear a name close to his and it puts me in panic mode. I shake my head and look over at Daphne, who is oblivious to my mini freak out moment. Daphne seems so put together compared to me. She told me her parents both died in a car accident when she was sixteen, and she lived with her older brother until she came to South University. She has plans to complete her bachelor's degree in nursing. She wants to be able to train other nurses someday. Things haven't been easy for her either, but she seems to be handling it well.

I glance back over toward the guys that just walked back and shake my head. I really am a mess. It's been almost three years and I can't get over my high school sweetheart. I roll over onto my stomach and get settled back on my towel. For the next hour Daphne and I lay there, flipping over every so often and visit with each other.

Sometime later Daphne and I are lying on our backs again with our eyes closed listening to the sounds around us. I hear footsteps in the sand near us; I open my eyes and see a guy wearing board shorts with a navy blue/light blue stripe design and a tight-fitting white shirt that shows off his muscular build. He is probably around six foot with light brown short wavy hair and is walking toward us. He stops in front of us wearing a cute smile. I prop myself up on my elbows and nudge Daphne. She looks over at me and follows my gaze. The guy is standing there with his charming smile checking us out. I lift my sunglasses up and raise my eyebrows at him, waiting for him to say something.

He looks over at Daphne. "So my buddies over there," he points toward a small group of guys, "bet me I wouldn't be able to start a conversation with the most beautiful girl on the beach. You wanna go out and get some drinks with their money tonight?" he says as he flashes a smile that probably has gotten him his way plenty of times.

Daphne and I burst out laughing. After a minute or two I begin to settle down and wipe the stray tears from under my eyes. I look up at this guy and he is still standing there smiling at us. I shake my head and ask, "Does that line really work for you? Do girls really fall for that?"

He chuckles and looks over at me, and I notice that he has light blue eyes. He shakes his head. "Would you believe me if I told you it's the first time I've used it?" He looks over at Daphne and winks.

I shake my head. "Nope."

He shrugs. "Well, it was worth a shot, right?"

He looks over at his friends, then back over at us, "So, where you ladies from? Tennessee? Because you're the only ten-I-see," he says with a Southern accent and a smirk.

Daphne and I burst out laughing again. This guy

can't be serious. By the look on his face he's just messing around with us and enjoying it.

"Ryan, are you harassing these ladies over here with your lame pick-up lines?"

"Nah, I'm just talking with them."

I look up and see another guy stop next to who I now know is Ryan. I can't make out the other guy's face because the glare of the sun.

"Right, so which one did he try to use this time?" I can hear the smile in his voice as he asks.

"Well, I guess he thought we were from Tennessee," Daphne says with a laugh.

He looks over at Ryan. "Really, Ryan? That is like the oldest one in the book." Then he turns back to us. "I apologize ahead of time for my friend here. He doesn't really know how to socialize with the ladies."

It's then that I get my first real glance at Ryan's friend, and I'm left speechless. I'm sure I look like a deer in the headlights as I sit there staring at Jayce Cooper. Ryan is Jayce's friend. Jayce's friend came over here and was hitting on us having no idea that he would be bringing my past with him.

Once the temporary shock wears off I take the time to study him. His hair is shorter like I noticed at the club. Up close now I can tell it's still the same color. His face has matured over the last few years and instead of being clean shaved it looks like he hasn't shaved for a day or two. He is wearing green and black plaid board shorts and a tight-fitting black shirt that shows just how much his body has changed. His chest has toned up and he has broader shoulders. I always thought he was good looking when we were younger, but now...wow! He looks gorgeous. I continue my way up to his eyes, the same dark chocolate brown eyes that I've missed so much, and realize they are staring back at me.

He begins studying me like I did him. As his gaze travels down my body I begin to see recognition in his eyes as he comes back up to my eyes. I don't know how much time has passed or what Ryan and Daphne are doing because I can't look away from Jayce. I notice as soon as Jayce begins to realize who I am and I know things aren't going to go well. I stand up and move a few feet from him.

"Elle..." he gasps. He steps toward me and begins to reach out to touch my face, but pulls back as if he's been burned. I begin to see the emotions running through him. Confusion. Relief. Love. Hurt. And the last one...anger.

Ryan takes Daphne by the hand and they begin walking a little way away mumbling something about giving us some privacy. They must have felt the tension and realized things were about to get awkward. Good judgement on their part.

I take a step toward him. "Jayce, I can explain...." I begin, but he steps back and cuts me off. "You can explain to me why I was told you were dead!" he scowls.

I knew he would be hurt and angry, but I guess part of me still always pictured that maybe someday if we saw each other it would be a happy reunion. Of course that was naïve of me to think that. This is definitely not the happy reunion I was hoping for. I don't even know where to begin, especially since he isn't even supposed to know I'm alive. I take a deep breath to begin but Jayce beats me to it.

He lets out a bitter laugh and shakes his head. "But you have been alive this whole time. Living your happy life here while everyone back in Oregon thought you were dead!"

Anger begins boiling up inside me. He's crossed the line now. I was far from living a happy life here. Yes, I've worked to start making things better, but I wouldn't say my life is happy. I understand that he was hurt, but so was I. "I didn't want to leave, Jayce!" I snap. My fists clench at my sides. "I didn't

have a choice! My life here has been far from perfect!"
I hiss. I take another step toward him, bringing me a
few inches from his face and look him in the eyes. I
stand there with my gaze locked on his. My anger
begins to dissolve as I stare into his eyes. "I loved
you, Jayce!" My voice breaks and tears begin to
stream down my face as I whisper, "I still do..."

His jaw clenches. "Why should I believe you?" I
look into his eyes and see he wants to believe. That
gives me a little hope.

I glance around and notice that some people are
staring our way. I lower my voice. "Jayce, can we go
somewhere else...please?" I beg.

"No," he says through clenched teeth. "We are
done here." My hope dissolves as he turns and walks
away. I stand there and watch him go with tears
running down my face. He has to know that I didn't
want to hurt him.

"Jayce! Wait!" I can't let him go without him
knowing everything. I run to catch up with him. He
stops but doesn't turn to look at me. I grab his arm
but he shrugs me off. I walk around to face him and
look up at him. "I know you're upset and I'll give you
time. I want to tell you everything. I need you to
know everything." I look down, then back up and
hesitate. "Can I please see your phone?"

He looks a little unsure, but reaches into his
pocket and hands me his phone. Although I could be
putting myself at risk I feel this is worth it. I put my
phone number into his phone and hand it back to
him. I grab his face and pull him down to mine and
place a kiss on his cheek. I glance into his eyes. "I've
never stopped loving you. You have to believe me.
Please give me a chance to explain everything. You
have my number now, so when you're ready..." Then
I turn and walk away. I don't say goodbye because
that would feel too final, and I'm not ready to let him
go.

I walk back over and begin packing up my things. I'm so distracted I don't notice Daphne come up next to me. "Hey," she says quietly, "I'll get the rest if you want to go get the car." I look up and smile sadly. "Thanks." I grab my bag and head toward the parking lot.

CHAPTER 6

Once back at the apartment I storm straight into my room. I'm not ready to talk about what happened at the beach. I get a change of clothes from my closet and head for the bathroom. I set my clothes on the counter and turn the water on for the shower. Once under the spray I close my eyes as I let the hot water run over me.

I stand there a few moments, and then I lose my strength and begin to cry. I can't hold it back anymore. Seeing Jayce up close made me realize just how much I missed him. I wanted him to wrap his arms around me and hold me like he did the last night we were together. I wanted him to tell me it would all be okay and we could fix this, but he didn't even want me to touch him. I hurt him so bad. No, I didn't just hurt him. I crushed him.

Realizing this makes me cry harder. I never meant for this to happen. I can't believe he thought I was dead this whole time. I never considered what he would be told or actually went through. I was so wrapped up in my own hurt that I didn't want to think about what it did to him. I didn't have a choice though and I needed him to know that. I wanted to be with him but couldn't because my safety and life was at risk.

The tears begin to slow as I feel a shimmer of hope. Jayce still loves me. I saw it when he looked at me. He was angry and hurt but that's because he doesn't know what really happened. I need to fix this, no matter what it takes. It's been over two and a half years and surely Frank the boss has moved on now. I have a new identity so it would take a lot to figure out where I am now. I'll give Jayce a few days to cool off, but if I don't hear from him then I will find him again. I won't lose him again.

With that decided I shut the water off and step out of the shower. I dry off and slip into a pair of pink sweatpants and a black baggy t-shirt. I run a brush through my hair and decide to leave it to air dry since I'm not going anywhere. With that I head to the living room to talk to Daphne.

I walk in and see Daphne sitting on the couch watching TV. She has already changed and it looks like she must've showered too since her hair is wet. I walk over and sit on the other side of the couch. We both sit there staring at the TV, neither of us saying anything.

I don't know how much time passes before Daphne begins to speak "So Ryan and I exchanged numbers. He wants to go out for drinks sometime before he leaves."

I turn and look at her, a little shocked. "Are you going to go?" I ask curiously.

"I don't know," she says with a hint of a smile. "Maybe."

I'm shocked because Daphne doesn't usually give out her number to guys that she just meets. In the time I have known her she has been on a few dates. The guys that she did date were from her classes and she had known them for a while. A grin spreads across my face. "It was the pick-up lines, wasn't it?"

She turns and tries to act offended. "No! If anything that would've turned me away."

I stare at her with a raised eyebrow and wait for her to continue.

She grabs the remote and turns the TV off. "Okay, okay. They were pretty funny in a cheesy kind of way, but no, that's not what got me to agree. Ryan and I began to realize that you and Jayce knew each other and there was history between you two. I mean, we could feel the tension coming off you guys. I realized that Jayce was your boyfriend from back home. We both knew you guys needed to talk in private so we went for a walk on the beach." She says with a smile, "At first we didn't say much. He eventually began telling me about himself. He has lived in Oregon his whole life. He grew up in Springfield, which is right outside of Eugene. His parents and twin sisters still live there and his sisters are seniors in high school. He met Jayce their freshman year at Oregon State University. They are both working toward their bachelor's in entrepreneurship. They are here with a group of friends from school for Spring Break. His parents own a house on the beach here so they came here since this week was going to be warmer. After that I told him a little about myself and then he asked if I'd like to go out for drinks before he leaves. I said maybe, we exchanged numbers, then I went to find you."

"Wow, I'm surprised," I chuckle.

She smiles and shrugs. "It's something spontaneous to do on break. He goes back to Oregon at the end of the week anyways." She watches me for a moment. "So did you and Jayce get things talked out?" she asks quietly.

I shake my head and look down. "Yes and no." She sits there and waits for me to continue. "I knew we left things unsaid and even knew I hurt him, but I didn't realize how bad. I think I didn't want to know. I tried to explain things to him but he wouldn't listen. I gave him my number and asked him to call me when he is ready so I can explain." I look over at her and shrug. "So now I just wait."

She nods her head and turns the TV back on and we begin watching. We don't talk any more about it the rest of the night. We eventually order take-out again and settle back on the couch to watch a movie. Afterward I turn in for the night. I'm exhausted and emotionally drained. I fall asleep right as my head hits the pillow.

***

The next morning when I wake up I call my mom. Last night I woke up in the middle of the night and did some thinking. I know Jayce and everyone was told that we were dead, but I want the details now. I need to know what he was told. I call my mom and let her know that I'm going to stop by. When I get off the phone I go get ready for the day. After I get dressed I walk into the kitchen and see a note on the table from Daphne saying she'll be spending the day with her brother. I pick up my keys off the counter, slip on my shoes, and walk out the door.

Fifteen minutes later I pull into my parents' drive. The house is white with navy blue shutters around the windows. It's a two bedroom, two bathroom ranch style house. Their house is nothing fancy, but they have upgraded some things over the past couple years and have turned it into a nice house for them.

As I begin to get out of my car my mom walks out the front door. "Hey honey." I shut the door and walk toward her.

"Hey Mom," I say as I give her a hug. I look a lot

like my mom. She has a small frame like me and is a couple inches taller. I got my honey color hair from her but she has dyed her hair a light brown since we moved here. The only real difference is our eye color, which I get from my dad. My dad and I have green eyes and hers are hazel.

"Let's go inside, I have lunch going," she says as she pulls back. We walk into the house and head straight for the kitchen. When we walk in my dad looks up and smiles. "Hey sweetie." My mom goes over to continue fixing lunch. I walk over and give him a hug. "Hey Dad." My dad isn't very tall, maybe about five-seven or so. He has brown hair that has begun to turn more gray over the past couple years.

Once my mom gets lunch done we all go eat in the dining room. We keep conversation light throughout the meal. I want to hold off on asking about what people were told until everything is cleaned up from lunch because I know it's going to be an emotional conversation. We finish eating and I help my mom clear the table and clean up the mess. I rinse all the dishes and put them in the dishwasher while she wipes off the table and counters. When everything is all done we all go sit in the family room.

I could make small talk again, but I decide to just ask the question that I've been thinking about since last night. I look at both my parents and ask, "What happened after we left Portland? Like, what happened with our house and what were people told?" They both look at each other then back at me, surprised by my question. I know they weren't expecting me to ask it. I never asked them before because I just wanted to try to get past it, but now I need to hear it.

My mom is the first to speak. "Where is this coming from, honey? You've never wanted to know before."

I look down at my lap because I don't want them

to read my expression. "I don't know. I've just been thinking about it lately and I'm curious now." I look back up and watch as my parents exchange a silent conversation. My mom nods and my dad speaks. "Riley, after we left our house that night it caught on fire." I gasp, shocked. My dad hesitantly continues. "They weren't able to make it to the house on time so everything got burned up in the fire. Since we were moved to witness protection the police took that opportunity to tell people that no one survived the fire. Everyone was told that we didn't make it."

"What caused the fire?" I ask quietly.

My dad hesitates and looks over at my mom. He looks back at me but won't meet my eyes. "They aren't sure what caused it." Then he looks away.

They are hiding something from me. I can feel it. If they weren't then my dad would be able to look me in the eye and tell me that they don't know, but he can't. "You're lying," I accuse, calling him out on it.

"Riley!" My mom gasps. "Don't talk to your dad like that."

"What? I can tell you guys are hiding something from me. I deserve to know."

My dad watches me closely. After a few moments he finally speaks. "You're right. I'm sorry. You deserve to know the truth. We didn't want to tell you because we were afraid you'd go backwards in all the progress that you have made in the past couple years. We were so worried about you those first few months here and we don't want you to regress."

He comes over to sit by me. I sit there quietly, waiting for him to continue. He catches my gaze to make sure I'm looking at him. "Riley, you remember how you dropped your purse at the gas station?" I nod and he continues. "Well, after you got away the guy found it as you know, and he took your driver's license. He looked up our address and came to our house that night. He was the one that burned our house down. He assumed you went home and was wanting to get you back for getting away and knowing that he murdered someone. When the police took him in he admitted to starting the fire. Of course at the time he believed you were in the house and that you didn't make it."

He sits quietly and waits for my reaction. A mix of emotions runs through me. I'm shocked that this guy would go after me like that, which shows me just how dangerous these men are. I'm sad because all our friends had to go through grieving us. I stand and begin to pace back and forth. I'm so angry. I'm angry he took everything away from me and my family in Portland.

"Why did I have to go to that stupid gas station? I should've just tried to make it home that night! That guy took *everything* from us! *Everything*! We lost our friends! I lost my boyfriend that I loved so much! We lost our life there!" My voice gets louder as I continue. "But no! That wasn't enough! He had to go to our house and burn it down so we would have nothing left!" I collapse on the floor and press my forehead against the carpet as I begin to sob. My parents come down on the floor next to me and hug me as I cry.

I don't know how much time passes but eventually I calm down and sit up.

"I know this has been hard for you, sweetie. It's been hard on all of us. You are so strong, and you have made a life for yourself. Your mom and I are very proud of you and how far you have come from all this." My dad pulls me into a hug and I hug him back.

"Thanks, Dad."

***

When I get home I decide I need to run. I'm still

angry about my house burning down and I need to do something. I usually do my kickboxing as my stress reliever, but since I don't have it today then I decide a good run will do. I change clothes, do a few stretches, and then head out.

When I get down to the lobby I put my ear buds in and let the music drown out everything. I walk outside and decide to run over by the college. As I begin to run toward the campus I have a strange feeling of being watched. I take a glance around but don't see anyone. There isn't very many people around and the ones that are aren't paying attention to me. Since I don't see anything I decide to just ignore it and continue running. I begin to focus on my strides and pick up my pace. As I build speed I start to focus on my breathing.

Breathe in.

I am Riley Lynn Anderson.

Breathe out.

I am not Elizabeth Grace Payton anymore.

Breathe in.

I am stronger now.

Breathe out.

I will make it through this.

After about thirty minutes of running I decide to head back to my apartment. I have a few more blocks left so I walk the rest the way for my cool down.

When I get a block away from my apartment I begin to have that strange feeling again. I casually look around and don't notice anyone paying attention to me. I see a few couples walking down one side of the street, and a few people by themselves walking away from me, but no one watching me.

As I walk up to the steps to my apartment the feeling is still there. I turn around and look down the street again but still don't see anything. I look across the street and glance around the parked cars on the street, but still nothing. Maybe hearing about how the fire got started is making me paranoid. I shrug and turn back around to go inside.

When I walk in Phil looks up and waves. I smile. "Hey Phil." He returns my smile and goes back to looking at his computer. I walk over to his desk and ask, "Anything exciting going on around here?"

He looks up and shakes his head. "Nah, not really. How was your run?"

I shrug. "It was okay." I glance around the lobby looking to see if anyone is watching me but there's no one there. "Well, I'll see you around, Phil." Phil nods and then glances back to his computer screen. I climb the stairs to my apartment on the third floor, unlock the door and walk in. Once inside I lock the door and go shower.

Afterward I put pajamas on and decide to spend the rest the night in my room watching movies. I was so exhausted from the past few days and my run that sometime during my second movie I dozed off.

CHAPTER 7

When I woke up this morning I knew I was going to have a hard time making it through the day. My legs were sore from my run yesterday but I still managed to make it out the door for my seven o'clock kickboxing class. After the forty-five minute long class I was ready to go home and soak in a hot bath. That wasn't an option though since I had to be to work at eight-thirty.

I was cutting it pretty close as I walked into the building right at eight-thirty. I ended up showering at the gym, so I was able to save a little time by not having to go home. I walk into the backroom and throw my things in my locker.

When I get back out to the front desk Sally one of the therapists looks up. "Hey Riley! How was your kickboxing?" Sally has blond curly hair down to her shoulders and pearl blue eyes. She is about five foot five and in great shape. Sometimes she goes to the kickboxing classes with me.

I walk over to my chair and log in to the computer, then turn to her. "It was good. I'm exhausted though. I thought last night it would be a good idea to go running so I was sore from that before I started kickboxing."

"Well, don't wear yourself out too much, otherwise we might be seeing you as a patient." She smiles and grabs some files. "Now get busy, missy, we have a lot to do today." Then she walks back to her office. I shake my head and laugh. Sally reminds me of a mother hen. She is a person that worries about others and enjoys taking care of other people, and I can't help but love her for it.

The rest of the day goes by fast. Sally wasn't kidding when she said we had a lot to do today. By the end of my shift I'm beat. I get my things from my locker and walk out to my car. Once I get in I pull out my phone and notice I have a few missed texts. Two of them are from Daphne, but I skip those because the other one is from a number with an Oregon area code. I sit there and just stare at it. It's been two days since I talked to him. I actually didn't think I would hear anything from him this soon because of how mad he seemed.

I click on the message and open it.

I'm ready to talk. Can you meet me where I saw you at beach the other day at 5 tonight?

I glance at the clock and see its four thirty-five. I won't have time to go home and change out of my work clothes but I don't care. I need to talk to him. I reply back that I will meet him there. Then I text Daphne back and let her know I'll be home later and drive to the beach.

***

I pull into the beach and park my car. I get out and look around. There isn't a lot of people here today, which doesn't surprise me since it's only in the low sixties. I grab my light zip-up from my backseat and put it on. I lock up my car and start walking over to our meeting spot. As I approach I look around and don't see Jayce yet, so I decide to sit down in the sand and wait. I close my eyes and just listen to the waves crash up onto shore.

I don't know how long I sit there, but I'm startled when someone taps me on the shoulder. My eyes shoot open and I turn around and see Jayce standing there. "Sorry, I didn't mean to scare you."

I stand up and brush the sand off my pants. "It's okay. I didn't hear you come up. I was, um..." I point out to the water, "just listening to the waves," I say nervously. Why am I so anxious? I try to calm myself down. This is Jayce, the guy that I've always been comfortable around and trusted. He won't be angry with me once he knows the truth. At least I hope he won't.

He looks out at the ocean, then back at me. "Yeah, you always did love the ocean." He turns and looks back out. I nod and go stand next to him.

We stand there side by side and just watch as the waves come in and crash on the shore. Reminds me of the old times when we were younger and would take day trips to the ocean. We always had a blast playing in sand, or just laying side by side talking and listening to the waves as they crashed on the shore. Back then times were good between us. Everything was perfect. Standing so close to him I'm tempted to reach over and take his hand, but I know now is not the time.

I glance over at Jayce. He must feel me looking at him because he glances back at me. "So you said you wanted to talk." His tone is flat and void of any emotion. I nod and sit down in the sand. I glance around to make sure no one else is around. Then I watch as Jayce takes a seat a couple feet away. Our eyes meet and he waits for me to begin.

I take a deep breath, "Do you remember when I left your house that last night? I told you I had to stop and get gas..."

He clenches his jaw. "Yeah, how can I forget? That was the last time I talked to you," he growls and looks away.

I put my hand on his arm and his body tenses, but I leave it there anyway. I wait for him to look at me. When he does I say, "Jayce, I know you're hurt and you're angry with me but please just give me a chance." He hesitates, and then nods and waits for me to continue.

"Well, on my way home that night I missed my turn. So I would've had to take the long way home. I stopped at a gas station in the rundown area of town. I went in to go pay for my gas after I talked to you. When I got inside no one was around that I could see."

Jayce watches me carefully now; he knows that isn't a safe side of town. "I heard a loud crash in the back so I went to see what it was. As I walked back I heard two men arguing. As I got closer I realized one guy was talking about the other guy owing him money. Well, the guy didn't have the money, so the other guy shot him." I look down and tears begin to fill my eyes. Talking about it is taking me back to that night. "Jayce, I saw him get shot." I shake my head as the tears begin to fall. "I was so scared! I tried to leave, but the guy saw me and grabbed me. I thought he was going to kill me. He told me he was going to take me to his boss." Chills run through my body as I remember the coldness in his eyes and I shiver. "I distracted him by getting him to talk while I grabbed my pepper spray out of my purse. I sprayed him with it and then ran. I got in my car and went straight to the police."

I didn't notice Jayce move next to me until he pulls my face to look up at him. He presses his forehead against mine. "I'm sorry, Elle! I'm so sorry!" He rubs his thumbs over my cheeks to clear the tears.

I shake my head and look up at him. "There's more..." I go on to explain the details up through the police questioning me, having me be a witness for the trial, and ending with how I got here.

Jayce and I sit there quietly. He doesn't say anything, and I can't tell by his expression what he is thinking. I reach over and grab his hand. He seems tense and his jaw is clenched. He looks over at me. "Jayce. Say something please..." I say quietly.

He stands up and begins to pace. I watch him go back and forth in front of me and wait. After a minute he stops and turns to face me. "Why didn't you contact me? Why didn't you tell me you were okay?" he snaps.

I sit there, speechless. He's mad at me?

He begins to pace again. "That morning I got to your house and saw that it had caught on fire. I panicked. I looked for you everywhere. After about an hour someone finally told me that you and your parents were killed in the fire." He stops and lets out a shaky breath and continues. "The police said they didn't know how it started but that no one made it out." Tears begin to fill his eyes and he shakes his head to try to clear them. "Do you know what I went through when I thought you were dead, Elle? I loved you! I was completely destroyed that day! I thought I was never going to see you again!" He looks away as a tear slips down his cheek. He wipes the tear off with his hand and looks down at me getting ready to say more, but I beat him to it.

I stand up with my fists clenched at my side and face him. "Do you think I wanted to go, Jayce?" I snap. "Were you not listening to what I just told you? I didn't have a choice! When I came here my parents didn't know what to do with me! I couldn't sleep because I had nightmares and woke up screaming if I did fall asleep! I would hardly eat and lost a bunch of weight! I was pretty much a zombie for the first few months! You weren't the only one suffering, Jayce!" I yell. "I loved you too!" I look away as tears begin to stream down my face.

Jayce steps toward me and brings my face up to look at him, but I look away.

"Elle, look at me."

I don't respond.

"Elle, please look at me," he pleads.

I look up and lock eyes with him. He cups my face with his hands and gently wipes the tears away. "Elle, I'm sorry. I wasn't mad at you. I understand you couldn't do anything and I know this isn't your fault." He shakes his head. "It's just hearing all that brought back all the memories of going to your house and thinking I lost you forever. It made me angry, but not with you. I just wish I could've been there for you. I wish you never had to go through any of that alone." He pulls me into a hug and rests his head on top of mine. "I'm so sorry, Elle," he whispers. I wrap my arms tightly around his waist and rest my head against his chest.

After a few minutes Jayce pulls away and steps back. He looks down at the ground, then back up at me. "So...um...you never told me your new name," he says quietly.

"Riley. Riley Lynn Anderson."

He nods. "I like it. It will be weird not calling you Elle though."

I look up at him and ask the question that I'm nervous to know the answer to. "Jayce, what happens now? What happens when you have to go back to Oregon?" I ask nervously as I bite my bottom lip.

He glances out at the ocean then back down at me. "Honestly, I don't know. I know we have a lot of things to talk about and work through, but I..." He pauses. "I can't lose you again, Riley."

"I don't want to lose you either," I say quietly.

"We'll figure out something. I'm here till Sunday, so if you're free we can hang out together and catch up."

I smile and nod. "I'd like that."

We stand there quietly, not really sure what to say. Things have become awkward since the hug. It's like neither of us knows what to say or how to act. One minute we want to go back to how things were before all this happened and then the next we realize that we are different people than we were before. We aren't really sure where we stand with each other. I don't even know if he has a girlfriend or not.

Jayce's phone dings, notifying him of a message, breaking the silence. He pulls his phone out and reads it, then puts it back in his pocket. He looks down at me. "That was my friends. They want to go do something tonight." He seems almost uncomfortable. "So I need to get going. I'm sorry."

I nod and begin walking toward our cars. Tears begin to fill my eyes but I refuse to let them fall. I don't want Jayce to see me cry over this. I don't even know why I'm upset. I know he's here with his friends and here to hang out with them, and I'm not upset about that. I just hate how awkward this is between us. Things were never weird like this.

"Riley, wait." Jayce catches up with me. He grabs my arm and turns me toward him. He scans my face. "Are you upset with me?"

I shake my head. "No, it's just things are...I don't know..."

"Awkward," he finishes for me and I nod. He continues, "I know, I'm sorry. I'm just unsure how to act. It's a lot to take in, you know? For the past few years I thought you were dead and that I would never see you again. I'm sure it's weird for you too—I mean, seeing me and thinking you would never get to again. We'll figure it out, Riley. Okay?" I look up at him and nod. "I'll walk you to your car."

We begin walking again in silence, and I get that now-familiar feeling of being watched. I glance around to see if I notice anyone nearby.

"Are you looking for someone?" Jayce asks.

"No." I continue scanning the parking lot, then look at Jayce. "Do you feel like someone is watching us?"

Jayce looks around and shrugs. "No, why? Do you?"

I nod. "Yeah. Yesterday I went for a run and felt the same thing, but when I looked around I couldn't see anyone." I shrug and try to play it off like it doesn't bother me. "Maybe I'm just being paranoid."

He looks unsure, as if he doesn't believe me. "Just be careful." I glance around one last time, still not seeing anything, then I nod.

We arrive at my car and I unlock my door. Jayce opens it for me. Before I get in he turns me toward him. "Hey, I meant what I said about figuring this out. I'm going to need some time to process all this but I will keep in touch. Okay?" I see the sincerity in his eyes.

"Okay," I smile back and get into my car to go home.

CHAPTER 8

Once I arrive inside my apartment I say hi to Daphne, then go straight to my room. Once there I change into a pair of black sweats and a white South University t-shirt.

When I get back to the kitchen I see Daphne cleaning up some dishes. She looks up when I walk in. "Hey, I just finished eating but there are some leftovers in the fridge. I wasn't sure when you'd be home."

"Thanks." I walk over and get them. After grabbing a plate I start dishing out some food. "So how was hanging out with your brother yesterday?" I put it in the microwave and then turn to her.

"It was good. We've both been busy and haven't had much time to hang out so it was nice to spend the day with him." She walks over and sits down at the table. "So how was hanging out with your parents?"

"It was good." Of course not really since I learned that my old house got burned down by the guy from the gas station, but I can't tell her that. "Then when I got home I went for a run over by campus and came home watched a couple movies and fell asleep." I take my food out of the microwave, get a water from the fridge, and go sit down at the table. I begin eating when Daphne asks, "So how'd it go with Jayce?" I'd texted her after work and let her know that I was meeting up with him.

"I don't know, Daph. Things are so awkward between us. It's like neither of us knows how to act. One minute it's like we are still together and then it's like we realize that things are different now and we don't know what to do or say."

"Do you want to be together?" she asks with a smile.

"Yes...no...I mean, I don't think that would even work. I live here and he is going back to Oregon, so I don't think that is really an option."

"People do long distance all the time, and you'll be done with your degree in May. So it would only be temporary."

I laugh. "What are you, Miss Matchmaker now? I know people do long distance, but it's just I don't think being together is an option. Plus I don't even know if he is with someone. I mean, for all I know he could have a girlfriend."

Daphne chuckles. "To answer your question, no, I am not a matchmaker, but I know you still have feelings for him. I saw it when you met him the other day and I could tell the same thing when he looked at you. Yes, there may be some unresolved issues that you need to work through but that's no big deal." She says it like it's so simple. "Also, to answer your other question—" She smiles mischievously.

"What question? What did you do?" I interrupt her.

"Jayce doesn't have a girlfriend."

I narrow my eyes at her.

"What? Ryan and I were talking and it kind of came up," she says innocently.

"It kind of came up?" I ask slowly, trying to hold back my irritation. It is not her business to get involved with Jayce and my issues. I mean, yes, she is my best friend, but still she had no right to ask Ryan questions like that about Jayce. Things are a lot more complicated then she knows, although I am glad to hear that Jayce doesn't have a girlfriend. Wait, it shouldn't matter to me if he does or doesn't anyway. I can't be with him because that puts him in danger and it's too risky.

She gets up and walks over to the cupboard to grab a cup, clearly trying to get out of this.

"What do you mean it kind of came up?" I snap, not able to hide the irritation any longer. Okay, I know this shouldn't be that big of deal, but I don't know what Ryan knows about me or if Jayce ever told him about me. I do know that if Ryan does know about me and that I was dead and now I'm alive, and if he told Daphne this then they are both going to have questions and get curious about everything. I'm not supposed to tell people the details. It's why I didn't try to make friends when we first came here because it makes things even more complicated. I have to walk on eggshells with everyone because I can't say too much. Now I have a best friend and was beginning to move on with my life, but now my past showed up. My past is mixing with my present, which should have never happened.

Daphne walks over to the fridge and pours some milk. "Well, we both saw how you and Jayce looked at each other that day and felt the tension between you two. You guys came up in conversation. I got curious and asked if Jayce had a girlfriend and Ryan told me. No big deal." She shrugs and smiles sweetly.

"So did Jayce tell Ryan anything about me?" I ask curiously. I know I just got mad at her for getting involved but now I need to know what he knows.

"Ryan said that Jayce has never mentioned

anything about you, but that Jayce has never really talked about his girlfriends. Do you want me to talk to Ryan and see if I can find out anything?"

"What? No! What is this, high school?" I laugh. "If I have questions about Jayce I'll ask him. So just let this matchmaker thing go, okay?"

"Yeah, of course," she says, then takes a drink from her cup to try to cover her smile.

"Daphne, I'm serious." I narrow my eyes at her.

She sets her cup down. "Fine."

"Good, so are you going to tell me about you and Ryan?" I smile.

"There isn't much to tell. We've talked a few times."

"You like him," I smirk.

She blushes. "What? No, I don't. Plus, he'll be going back to Oregon soon."

"Long distance relationships work all the time," I mock. "Isn't that what you told me?"

"Whatever, Riley! I don't like him. He's just fun to talk to, that's all." She shrugs, trying to play it off cool. But I'm not buying it; I can see it in her eyes. I let it go because she'll just keep denying it.

"Okay, okay. I'll let it go," I laugh. I take my plate to the sink and clean up my mess. After I get my dishes washed and things put away I walk into the family room where Daphne moved. I sit by her on the couch and spend the rest of the night watching a movie.

***

Today had been a long day at work. There wasn't a lot going on so the day just seemed to drag. I was definitely ready to leave when the clock hit five. I still hadn't heard from Jayce, which I'm not too surprised about. I know it's all a lot to take in, and I'm sure a big shock to know that I'm not dead. I just hope he doesn't wait too long because he'll go back to Oregon soon. I don't know what will happen then. All I know is I want to spend as much time with him as possible while he is here, but I'll have to wait to see what he wants to do.

When I get home Daphne comes out of her room. "How was work?" She walks over and leans against the counter.

I set my things on the table and collapse in the chair. "It was long. I felt like the day was never going to end. Definitely glad to be off."

She beams. "Good! That means you'll be ready to go out tonight then. You know, go out and have some fun."

"Actually that does sound nice and I don't have to work tomorrow." I think going out would be the perfect distraction I need to get my mind off Jayce. "Who's going?"

"Just me and you."

"Sounds good. I'm going to go lay down for a bit." I begin walking back toward my room. "What time are we leaving?" I call over my shoulder.

"Be ready at nine!"

***

I must've been really tired because I didn't wake up until my phone alarm went off at eight. I check my phone, and still no messages from Jayce. Thankfully I'm going out tonight so I won't be tempted to check my phone all night. I roll out of bed and go take a shower. Afterward I get changed into a pair of black skinny jeans and a teal top. I decide to blow dry and straighten my hair tonight. Once I have my hair fixed I put on some black eyeliner, black mascara, and a little bit of eye shadow.

"Riley, it's time to go!"

"Coming." I go into my room, check to make sure

I have my ID, and head out to meet Daphne.

I enter the living room as Daphne walks out of her room. She is wearing dark jeans with a red off the shoulder top and black pumps. Her hair is in loose waves, which hangs down to the middle of her back. She walks over to the door. "You ready to go?" I nod and walk out with her.

We walk into the club which is already beginning to fill up and go straight to the bar. The club has a big dance floor in the middle with tables and chairs around it. Stairs go up to a second level that overlooks the dance floor with tables and chairs as well. There are a couple pool tables along the back wall which are already in use.

After squeezing up to the bar and getting our drinks we head over to a table. I'm not really paying attention to where we are going and just let Daphne lead the way. Once we stop I look up and see Ryan and Jayce sitting there drinking their beers. Jayce looks just as surprised to see me. I look over to Daphne and narrow my eyes. "Daphne, what is going on?"

She looks guilty. "Well, I knew if I told you we were meeting Ryan and Jayce then you wouldn't have come so..." She trails off. She's right. I wouldn't have agreed to come out because Jayce said he wanted some space. I know she means well but I already told her she needed to stay out of this and quit playing matchmaker. I turn and begin walking away. I know I'm acting immature, but this past week has brought up memories and emotions I thought I was moving on from and I don't know how to handle it.

"Riles! Wait!" Daphne calls out after me, but I just keep walking. I don't want to talk to her right now because I'm mad. She went behind my back and set this up. I just wanted to come out with my friend, have a good night and pretend my life was somewhat normal. I weave through the people and head for the bathroom. Once I'm in the bathroom I take my drink and chug it. I lean against the wall for a minute and let the alcohol begin to run through my body.

Deciding I'm not going to let this ruin my night, I walk out of the bathroom and head over to the bar for another drink. Two shots. Probably not the wisest choice, but I'm hoping the alcohol will help settle my nerves. I down my shots and head over to the door that leads to the patio.

Once I'm outside I walk over to the far side and lean against the wall. I close my eyes and take a deep breath.

"Riley?"

I open my eyes and look over to the left and see Jayce sitting one table over from where I'm leaning against the wall. Wonderful. I was trying to avoid them for at least awhile until I got myself back under control. I begin to walk away when Jayce reaches out and grabs my arm. "Are you okay?"

"I'm fine." I turn to face him, "I'm sorry, I didn't know you were going to be here tonight. Daphne told me it was just going to be us. If..."

"Riley, its fine. Ryan told me the same thing, which irritates me that he lied to me. You can sit out here with me if you want to." I look up and see the sincerity in his eyes. I start to hesitate because I know he said before he wanted space.

He must see the hesitation on my face because he adds softly. "Please."

I nod. "Okay."

I start to walk over to sit down next to him but my foot gets caught on the leg of a chair. I start to fall but Jayce reaches out and catches me around the waist.

He stands me upright and looks down at me with amusement. "Still clumsy I see," he chuckles.

"I may be a little tipsy too," I giggle. He laughs as

he steps back and pulls out the chair for me.

We both take our seats and he begins drinking his beer. We sit in silence for a few minutes. I look around and see we are the only ones out here. I glance over at Jayce and notice he's watching me. After a moment he asks, "Do you remember that time that me and you tried to set Olivia and Evan up?"

"Yes, they were so mad at us for that," I laugh. When we were seventeen Jayce and I had this brilliant idea that we would all go to a movie together. I told Olivia it would just be me and her, and Jayce told Evan it would just be the two of them. Sound familiar? Well, Olivia and I got to the theater first and went to get drinks and popcorn. We started walking back toward our theater and saw Jayce and Evan walking toward us. When Olivia and Evan realized what was going on they were furious with us. Olivia was glaring at me and Evan was growling at Jayce.

"I think the funniest part of that night was when Olivia dumped the popcorn all over Evan." Jayce shakes his head and laughs. "And Evan's expression?" He chuckles. "Priceless."

I laugh along with him thinking about it. Jayce and Evan had stopped in front of us, then Jayce took my hand and we began walking toward our theater, ignoring our friends' expressions. After a few steps we both glanced back and saw Olivia dump her popcorn on Evan then she stomped past us to the theater. Evan just stood there shocked for several moments, then he looked at us and asked, "What just happened?" Jayce and I busted out laughing. When I asked Olivia about it later she just shrugged and said, "He deserved it."

Jayce laughs bringing me back to the present. "I guess we know how Olivia and Evan felt."

I begin to feel awkward. Does that mean he doesn't want me to be here and he's mad that I am?

"Do you want me to leave?" I ask hesitantly.

He looks over at me. "No, of course not. I just think it's funny that Daphne and Ryan did what we did to Olivia and Evan. I'm kind of glad though because I was actually going to call you to see if you would want to hang out tomorrow night." He gives me his charming smile. "Do you have plans tomorrow?" He knows I can't say no to that smile.

"No, I don't have any plans," I smile back.

Jayce and I decide for him to pick me up at seven and go out to dinner. After that we begin to catch up. I tell him about my job and about finishing up my degree this semester. He tells me about how he is going to Oregon State University and is on his third year working toward his entrepreneurship degree with just one more year left. It's good to hear that he went to college and began working toward what he wanted after I left. I'm glad to know that my leaving didn't stop him from that. He said that he almost didn't go but his parents kind of pushed him into it. They said that I would want him to move forward and go to college, and they were right. I wanted him to move on and be happy.

"So how are Olivia and Evan?" I'm curious to know if they are still friends and how they are doing with everything. I miss being able to see them. We always did so much together.

"They are doing well. They both are still going to OSU. Evan and I got an apartment together after freshman year. Olivia and a girl from one of her classes got an apartment shortly after we did." Jayce shifts in his seat a little and looks away. "We don't really hang out with Olivia that much, honestly. We still keep in touch...well, she and I do mainly. She and Evan still haven't resolved anything." He shakes his head and takes a sip of his beer. "I don't know if they ever will," he chuckles.

"Did they come out here with you?"

"No, they both had other plans for Spring Break."

"Have you told anyone about me?" I look over at him.

"No, I've wanted to tell Evan and Olivia but I know I can't."

I nod. "I miss them," I whisper. My eyes begin to tear up just thinking about them. We all used to be so close and now since I'm gone it's like our group fell apart.

I look up when Jayce grabs my hand. "I know, Riley. I'm sorry. I know they miss you too." I nod and look away as a tear slips down my cheek. I wipe it away before Jayce sees, frustrated that I keep crying so much.

Jayce pulls me up. "It's getting late. I'm ready to head out, are you? I can give you a ride home."

"Sure." I pull out my phone and text Daphne to let her know I'm leaving, then we head out toward the parking lot.

CHAPTER 9

When we arrive at my apartment Jayce comes around to my side of the car and opens the door for me. He holds out his hand to help me out. "Thanks," I say as I place my hand in his. He pulls me out and shuts the door. We walk up to my apartment in silence and I realize he is still holding my hand. When we get to my door I reluctantly let go of his hand and find my keys. Once I have them I look up and notice his intense gaze on me.

"Thanks for bringing me home," I say bashfully. I feel like this is high school all over again and it's my first date or something. I'm so nervous and I'm not sure how to act.

"No problem." He puts his hands in his pockets, and I notice that he looks nervous too. Glad to know I'm not the only one. We stand there just looking at each other. Here in the light I notice how good he looks tonight. He's wearing dark denim jeans with a white long-sleeved Henley shirt. He definitely filled out. I look up at him and by the smirk on Jayce's face he knows I was just checking him out.

He takes a step closer to me. He reaches up,

brushes a piece of hair off my face and tucks it behind my ear and I shiver in response. He glances down at my mouth then back up to my eyes.

"Riley, are you seeing anyone?" His voice is husky and low. I must have a confused look on my face because he clarifies, "A boyfriend?" I shake my head.

He nods and leans down. "Good."

Before I can respond Jayce's lips are on mine. I'm stunned for a moment because I was not expecting Jayce to kiss me. Before I can kiss him back he pulls away and rests his forehead on mine. "I had to do that. I've wanted to do that all night. I've missed you so much. I'm so sorry I wasn't there for you when you went through all that stuff. And I'm sorry I acted like a jerk these last couple times I saw you. I just..."

I put my finger to his lips to stop him. "Jayce, I get it. I've missed you too."

Jayce leans down and presses his lips to mine in a sweet, tender kiss. I wrap my arms around his neck and return his kiss this time. He walks us back until I hit the wall. Wrapping his arms around my waist, he pulls me closer as he deepens the kiss.

All the feelings that I've tried to let go come crashing into me full force. I've missed this so much. I've missed him holding me. I've missed kissing him. I've missed just spending time with him and talking. He wasn't just my boyfriend, he was my best friend. What am I going to do when he leaves? I don't want to lose him again. Being in contact isn't okay, which is exactly why I haven't told my parents. I push that thought out of my mind and grab his shirt, trying to pull him closer.

I don't know how much time passes when Jayce breaks the kiss. He leans his forehead against mine. "I need to get going, otherwise I won't be able to leave." I nod, trying to catch my breath. "I will be here tomorrow night at seven to pick you up."

"Okay,"

"Goodnight, Riley." He presses his lips to my forehead, lingering there for a moment longer.

I look up into his dark chocolate eyes that I have missed so much and can't help but smile. "Goodnight, Jayce." Grabbing his face I gently pull him down and place a kiss on his lips. I pull back and see him smiling back at me.

Unlocking my door and walking into my apartment is one of the hardest things I've ever done. Peeking around the door before I shut it, I watch Jayce walk away. Once he's out of sight I lock the door and lean back against it, my hand reaching up to touch my lips.

The night definitely turned out differently than I thought it would. When I first saw Jayce at the club tonight I thought he would be mad; he wanted space, after all. I was mad at Daphne for lying to me, and I planned on having some words with her later. I guess her plan worked out in the end anyway, because Jayce and I were both irritated with Ryan and Daphne so they got to spend the evening alone together. A smile crosses my face as I think about sitting out on the patio just talking and catching up with Jayce. It was so nice, and things weren't awkward.

My cheeks warm as I think about the kiss out in the hallway. It was like we couldn't get enough of each other. If Jayce didn't break the kiss things probably would've been taken further. He definitely had more control than I did. I probably would've asked him to come in, which we aren't ready for yet. We still have things we need to figure out, like what happens when he leaves.

That thought snaps me back to reality. What am I doing? I can't get attached to him. He is going to be going back to Oregon, and I can't go with him. Plus, I could get relocated at any time. Then I would end up breaking his heart and my heart all over again. My eyes begin to fill with tears. I swipe at them and push off the door and storm into my room. I'm angry with myself for believing Jayce and I could have a happy ending together.

After changing and getting ready for bed I turn off my bedroom light and crawl beneath the covers. Lying there I realize what I'll have to do. I need to text Jayce and cancel our plans. There's no way I can go out with him tomorrow. I'll be too tempted to continue things with him and that can't happen. I decide to wait until morning and begin to drift off to sleep.

***

The next morning I awake to the front door being shut. Interesting. I roll out of bed, peek out my door and see Daphne. She is still in her clothes from last night but her hair is thrown up in a messy bun. Really interesting. I open my door and make sure that it hits the wall. Startled, Daphne jumps and looks over at me. "Jeez, Riley, you scared me!"

"You just get home?" I ask innocently.

She blushes. "Um…yeah."

I smirk. "Did you happen to stay with Ryan last night?"

She turns redder and looks away knowing she's been caught. I can't let her out that easy, not after what she pulled last night with Jayce and me.

"You did, didn't you?" She doesn't answer, which only confirms it. I'm actually a little surprised. I knew she liked him, but this isn't something she normally does. Since I've known Daphne, she's never gotten serious with guys and she definitely hasn't stayed the night with a guy. She's never said anything but sometimes I wonder if she had a bad experience with an ex-boyfriend, and that's why she keeps her distance.

She finally looks over at me. "It just sort of happened. We were having a good time at the club, but it was hard to visit there. So we decided to go back to his place since Jayce was bringing you home. We figured we'd give you some time." With a shrug she continues. "We stayed up for a while talking and then eventually we both fell asleep together on the couch." Big sigh. "Riley, what do I do? This isn't me." Daphne laughs a little with a shake of her head. "You know I don't get involved with guys. I like to keep things simple and relationships complicate things."

"I don't know, Daph. I'm probably the last person that should be giving you advice," I laugh.

"Listen, about last night..." I begin to say, but Daphne holds up her hand to stop me.

"I'm sorry I lied to you about just being us girls. I know I said I was done playing matchmaker but Ryan and I thought you guys just needed a little push to get past the awkwardness. I wasn't trying to upset you." A smile creeps across her face. "From what it sounds like our little plan must've worked since he brought you home and we didn't see you guys all night."

With a giggle I reply, "Yes, I was mad at you for lying to me. But I guess I should say thank you because I think last night helped a little bit. Things weren't as awkward and we actually talked and got to catch up, which was nice."

She raises an eyebrow. "And? I know there is more. I see it in your eyes."

I shake my head. "And we kissed. And he is supposed to take me out tonight."

"Yah! I'm excited for you!" Daphne squeals.

I interrupt her excitement with, "But I'm canceling."

"What do you mean you're canceling?"

Plopping on the couch, I lay my head against the back and stare at the ceiling. "I'm not going to go out with him. I can't, Daph."

She crosses over and sits next to me. "Um...and why not? This is your second chance."

I look over at her. "There is no second chance for us. We can't be together. He will be going back to his life in Oregon and I will continue living my life here. It will only make things harder if we continue spending time together while he is here."

"But..."

"No! I'm not changing my mind on this so don't try to fix this," I snap. I know I'm being harsh but I need her to stop pushing. I meet her gaze again and sigh. "Look, Daph I'm sorry. I know you think this will work but I need you to let it go. For real this time. Please."

She shakes her head in resignation. "Fine. I'll stay out of it this time. I just don't want to watch my best friend walk away from something that could be great." She gives me a sad smile.

"I know. Thanks. I'm going to go shower." I get up off the couch and go to my room.

I walk over to my bed and fall back. Staring at the ceiling, I lay there wondering if I'm doing the right thing. I mean, what would be the point in spending the rest of break together if once he goes back to Oregon I can't have contact with him? I really shouldn't even be contacting him now, but I needed him to know what really happened. Especially after he saw me. There were so many times when we first got here that I just wanted to call him just to hear his voice. I even began dialing his number several times but would always talk myself out of it. At the time I never knew what I would say to him.

The day at the beach when I saw him up close I knew I needed to tell him everything. I couldn't have him leave without knowing the truth. I told him everything and now I need to let him go so he can go back to his life in Oregon. I grab my phone off my nightstand and send Jayce a text.

Me: *Hey, tonight isn't going to work. I'm sorry.*

I'm surprised when I get a text back right away.

Jayce: *Ok, what about tomorrow night?*

I have a feeling he isn't going to make this easy. Instead of replying I don't respond. I know its mean, but I'm not going to explain everything over text. And I know if I talk to him on the phone I won't be able to say no to him. This is hard enough as it is.

Instead of showering I decide I need to go for a run. I skipped kickboxing this morning since we went out last night and now I need something to get my mind off everything. I toss my phone on my bed, get a pair of shorts and a t-shirt and go into the bathroom to change. After I put my hair up I walk into my room and put on my running shoes. Once I have my phone and earbuds I walk into the kitchen. I don't see Daphne, so I assume she is in her room. I decide to leave her a note letting her know I'm going out for a bit just in case she comes looking for me, then I leave.

CHAPTER 10

After my run I wasn't ready to go up to my apartment, so I got in my car and drove to the beach instead. I park, get a towel from the backseat, and walk toward the beach. Once I find a spot away from the few groups of people that are here I lay out my towel and sit down.

It's beautiful out. The skies are clear and there is a light breeze coming off the ocean. It's probably about seventy-five degrees. I lean back against my hands and close my eyes as the salty air brushes across my face and the waves crash against the shore. I could stay out here forever. Being on the beach and listening to the ocean is so soothing.

During the summers back in Portland Jayce and I used to spend a lot of days at the beach. It was only an hour and a half drive so we would head out in the morning and spend the day there. Sometimes we would go, just us, and sometimes we would meet other people there. The water temperature was never warm enough to actually swim but it was still a lot of fun to go. Living here I have been able to enjoy the beach a lot more and I love it. That's made moving here a little bit easier. I came out here to think a lot or when I was struggling with things. Sometimes I would just come here to sit and listen to the ocean for hours. There is just something about it that helps calm me.

I'm brought out of my thoughts when I hear someone approach. As the person gets closer I know who it is without looking. I continue to lean back against my hands with my eyes closed. The person sits down next to me. "I knew you'd be out here," he says quietly.

I open my eyes and look over. Jayce is sitting in the same position as me and looking out at the ocean. He's wearing a white t-shirt and navy board shorts. Inwardly, I sigh. He always looks good in whatever he wears. It's still weird seeing him here, but I could never get tired of it.

"Are you stalking me?" I tease.

He glances over and I see the corners of his mouth twitch. "No, but you're pretty predictable. I figured I'd find you here." He looks back out to the ocean and we sit in silence just watching the waves come in.

After a few minutes he asks, "So are you going to tell me the reason you cancelled our plans tonight and why you were planning on just ignoring me?"

Even after all this time he still knows me. Unless..."Did you hear that from Ryan or Daphne?" I look over at him.

"No, Riley. I just know you. You're scared so you're pushing me away."

"Of course I'm scared. I'm not supposed to have contact with people from before. It puts all of us at risk. I don't know what would happened if they found out. They could send us away again and give us new identities. I don't know, but Jayce, I can't go through that again. I can't make my parents go through that again either. I've put them through enough."

Jayce touches my arm. "Hey. This isn't your fault. You know that, right?" He looks over at me with concern.

"I know that." I shake my head. "But what I'm trying to say is it's too risky to keep in contact. So I think its best just to let each other go now before either of us gets hurt." I look out to the ocean, trying to stay strong in my decision.

"You're joking, right? Look, I know you're scared, but there is still something between us. Last night confirmed it for me even before we kissed, and I know you feel it too. I know I have to go back to Oregon but while I'm here I want to spend time with you. We can figure out details later." He grabs both of my hands and turns me to face him. "Riley, please don't push me away. Let me spend time with you while I'm here."

I look down at our hands. He is right. There are still feelings between us. Even after all this time my feelings for him haven't changed. Is it weird to still love someone that you have been away from for almost three years? I don't know, but either way I do. I still love him. I know I should tell him no and walk away but I can't. This is why I didn't respond back to his text and why I wanted to avoid him, because I knew I would give in. Apparently I want to have my heart broken again because that is what will happen when he leaves, but I'll deal with that when the time comes. He's here with me now and I'm going to take what I can get.

I look up into his eyes and can see that he's nervous I'm going to say no. A slow grin begins to spread across my face. "Okay."

A huge smile spreads across his face and he pulls me into his lap. His hands find the sides of my face. "Good." Jayce gives me a kiss on the forehead. "So what do you have planned for the rest of the day?"

"I didn't really have anything planned. I need to go home and shower before we do anything. I went for a run and then came straight here." I glance down and realize I must look awful. "I probably smell pretty bad." I scrunch my nose up and begin to climb off his lap.

He laughs and stops me. "You're fine. How about we hang out here for a while, then I'll go back to my place and get ready while you go home and shower?"

"That sounds good." Jayce lifts me off his lap and sets me down next to him. He makes lifting me seem so effortless. I sit back on my hands. "So I'm curious. What does Ryan know about me, or me as Elizabeth?"

He looks over at me. "I haven't told him much. He knows about both but thinks they are different people. I've told him that I had a girlfriend named Elizabeth that died in a fire back in high school. Then I told him that you and I have history, but that is all I've told him. There have been times that I've almost slipped, calling you Elle instead of Riley."

I nod. "I'm sorry that I've put you in this position. It's hard when Daphne asks me questions about us too. She thinks I moved with my parents from Iowa. She knows that we have a history, but I don't know what I'm going to do if she learns that you grew up in Oregon. Then I know she'll have questions and I don't know what to tell her." I shake my head. "My life is a mess." I laugh.

"Riley, don't apologize to me. You didn't do anything wrong. As far as Ryan I won't tell him about your situation. With Daphne, I don't know what you should tell her."

"All right, let's talk about something else," I say with a smile. I don't want to talk about what a mess I'm in anymore. He agrees and we begin talking about things we have been up to these last couple years. We talk about friends, school, and our parents. It feels just like old times, sitting here on the beach and talking. We've never brought up the subject of exes, and I'm not sure I'm ready to hear if or how many girls he's dated. It's still too sensitive of a subject right now.

We stay at the beach for a couple more hours, and then head back to our own places to get showered and ready to go out. When I get to my apartment I decide on a white cotton strapless sundress with a green flower design all over it a black shrug to go over it. I leave my hair down with loose curls. As I put on a light layer of eye makeup and apply my lip gloss I hear a knock on the door.

"Riley! Your date is here!" Daphne yells from the family room. Of course she is going to give me crap about this. I don't even know if this is a date. I mean, I think it is, but I don't know for sure. I walk into my room and grab my things, including a pair of jeans and top just in case.

When I came home from the beach earlier Daphne noticed that something had changed. She told me I looked happier, and then after about five minutes of her bugging me I gave in and told her that Jayce was taking me out. She of course squealed and did a happy dance of some sort. When she finally calmed down I told her not to get too excited because we just agreed to spend time while he was here and hadn't figured out anything beyond that. She of course just waved me off.

Daphne is sitting on the couch when I walk through the living room and she counters my glare with a grin. Part of me wants to walk over and throw a pillow at her face. I open the door and there standing on the other side is Jayce. When he hears the door open he looks up and smiles. "Hey." That sweet expression could melt me into a puddle right here.

"Hey," I smile back at him. It's tenth grade all

over again and he's picking me up for our first date. His eyes roam over me from my head down my legs, and back up. "Wow! You look..." He steps closer and looks down at me. "You're gorgeous."

"Thank you," I reply with a shy smile. He pulls my hand up and brings it to his lips. "Are you ready to go?" I look up at him and nod. As I'm pulling the door closed Daphne yells, "Have her home by midnight!" I hear her laugh as I close the door. I'm going to get her back somehow.

Jayce laughs as he grabs my hand. We walk down to his car and he opens the passenger side for me to get in. Once we're inside he looks over at me, "Where do you want to go eat?"

"There's a tavern that we could go to about ten minutes from here." He nods. "Sounds good." He hands me the GPS and I type the address in. I always loved that about me and Jayce. We both didn't need to go anywhere fancy to eat; not that we never went to fancier places. We just preferred going somewhere casual. We don't talk much on the drive, instead just listening to country tunes from the radio.

When we pull into the tavern Jayce gets out and comes around to open my door. He reaches out a hand for me and I look up and smile as I take it. He helps me out and places his hand on the small of my back as we walk toward the restaurant.

Once we get inside we are seated at a booth in the back corner. A minute later a waitress comes up "Hi, I'm Molly. I'll be your waitress this evening. What can I get you to drink tonight?" I glance up from my menu and notice that Molly is beaming at Jayce. I watch as her gaze roams over him, checking him out. Jayce is oblivious to this and is studying the menu. Molly is probably around eighteen and a skinny five foot six with shiny dark brown hair that falls down to the middle of her back. Her makeup is a little overdone but still she is really pretty.

"I'll have a water, please." She glances over at me and forces a polite smile, then looks back over at Jayce "And for you?" she asks sweetly.

Jayce glances up and orders a beer, then looks back down at his menu. Molly nods and stomps away. Once she's gone, I begin laughing and Jayce looks up from his menu. "What's so funny?"

"Our waitress was totally checking you out and you were completely oblivious to it. She didn't like it at all. She just stomped away."

He shrugs and sets his menu down. "I'm not interested. I'm here with you." He grabs my hands and looks into my eyes. "And you I am interested in." By the look in his eyes I know he truly means that. He brings my hands up and places a kiss on each one, then places our hands back down on the table. My cheeks turn a shade of pink at his intense stare.

Our waitress Molly walks over and sets our drinks down in front of us, breaking our moment. She glances from Jayce to me then back to Jayce, a look of disappointment passing over her face but she masks it with a smile. "Are you guys ready to order yet?"

Jayce and I both order cheeseburgers and fries, and Molly walks away to go place our orders. I guess she got the hint that we were actually here together. At least she didn't continue to try to get his attention. I hate when people do that.

I look over at Jayce. "So who all came here with you to Virginia?"

"Just four of us. Ryan, who you've met. Then the two other guys are Spencer and John. They're Ryan's roommates. I'm not as close with them but we all hang out sometimes. They're pretty cool."

"Were they mad that you were coming to hang out with me again?" I don't want to cause problems between him and his friends. I mean, they all came here together and I don't want to take away from their guy time or whatever.

Jayce chuckles, "Nah, they don't care. We can always hang out when we get back."

I nod. "I just wanted to make sure I wouldn't create problems with you guys."

"No worries," Jayce assures.

A few moments later Molly brings us our food. "Is there anything else I can get for you?" She glances between the two of us as we shake our heads. "No, thank you," I say.

Once she leaves we dig into our food. We don't talk much as we eat. Once we finish and the waitress brings us the bill, we leave the money on the table and head out. When we get to the car Jayce opens the door for me once again.

"So what would you like to do?" he asks when he gets in the car.

"Am I boring if I say I don't really want to go out somewhere?"

He chuckles and shakes his head. "No, you never did like going out places." Jayce hesitates and looks over at me. "I can take you home if you want."

"Would you want to go walk on the boardwalk?" I don't want to be boring but I'd rather go somewhere where it's just us so we can visit if we want. Going out to the bars and clubs makes it harder to have conversations. Plus, it hasn't cooled down too much.

He smiles. "Sounds great."

CHAPTER 11

We arrive at the beach fifteen minutes later. I look out the window and don't see too many people out on the boardwalk. A few couples and groups of people are off in the distance. Glancing around us I don't see anyone close by. Perfect. I grab my clothes and unbuckle my seatbelt. I look over at Jayce, and see he is watching me with raised eyebrows.

"I brought a change of clothes because I wasn't sure what our plans were." I glance down at my clothes then back up at him. "I wanted to change before we go on a walk."

"Okay. Where did you want to change at?"

I look around outside the car again and still don't see anyone. "Well, since no one is around I was going to change in your car. Can you stand guard outside?"

He stares at me like I've lost my mind. "You're going to change in the car? Right here?"

"Yeah, no one is around." I laugh as he just stares are me. "Jayce, just go."

He hesitates for a moment then nods. After getting out he begins to shut the door. "And no peeking, Jayce!" I call.

He turns around and smirks. "It's not like I haven't seen you before," he reminds me with a wink.

I sit there, stunned, my face turning red. I can't believe he just said that. It isn't a lie, but that was several years ago.

Jayce laughs at my expression. "What? I've seen you in a bikini. What did you think I meant?" Yeah, we both know that's not what he was talking about. I'm about ready to tell him that but he shuts the door, then he knocks on the window and motions for me to hurry up. I glare at him and motion for him to turn around. He laughs harder as he turns and leans his back against the door.

Grabbing my jeans, I slip them on and pull them up under my dress. Next my shrug gets tossed in the backseat. I put my shirt on over my dress and reach back and unzip my dress. Completely covered, I pull my dress off. I fold it up and put it in the backseat with my shrug, grab my purse and get out of the car. Jayce looks over. "You ready to go?"

I nod. Jayce begins to walk around to my side of the car and stops. "Do I need to worry about you smacking me?" he chuckles.

I shrug. "I'm not making any promises."

He continues walking over to me, then stops in front of me and places his hands on my waist. Leaning down and placing his mouth by my ear he whispers, "You walked right into that comment, Riley." His breath brushes across my neck and my body tingles in response. He pulls back and smiles knowing the effect he still has on me. Letting go of my waist and grabbing my left hand, we begin walking toward the boardwalk.

I look up and notice there are a lot more people on the boardwalk than I saw before. I pull Jayce to a stop. He looks over at me, confused.

"Do you want to walk along the beach instead?"

He glances up at the boardwalk ahead and then back at me. "Yeah, that's fine." We begin walking toward the beach in silence. I look across the beach and see just a few people walking along but in the opposite direction.

After a few moments of walking Jayce breaks the silence first. "So what are your plans once you finish your degree this semester?"

"I'm not really sure, honestly. The place I work at isn't hiring for a physical therapist assistant at the moment," I shrug. "I'll probably continue working there for now. I enjoy the people I work with and they already told me when I get done with school they could make me full time."

When I first started my job I only talked to people when I had to. I didn't start conversations; I tried to avoid them. Now that I've worked there two years I'm familiar with the people and feel comfortable around them. Since being in Witness Protection I don't like meeting new people. I prefer to be around the people I know now. At school I still don't really talk to anyone except Gavin and Daphne. I don't want to have to start over somewhere else.

Jayce nods. "That's good."

"What about you? What are your plans when you get done with school next year?" I don't really want to have this conversation because then it makes me think about him not being here, but I am curious to know what he has planned.

"I haven't really thought ahead that far. I know I want to run my own business someday. I've thought about getting a management job at a bigger company first just to get a feel for things. I don't know though, I still have another year. A lot can happen in a year," he smiles down at me. The way he's looking at me makes me wonder if there is a bigger meaning to that statement but I decide not to think too much into it.

"So Ryan asked if we would want to go out with

him and Daphne tomorrow night. I think Spencer and John might come too. Would you want to go?"

"Yeah, that sounds fun."

We walk in silence for a while, but it's not awkward anymore. As we walk I keep going back to wondering if Jayce dated anyone over these past couple years. I want to know if he moved on, or tried to. I would think that he would've. I mean to him I was gone forever.

Curiosity gets the best of me and I decide to ask. "Jayce?"

I continue gazing ahead but I can feel him turn to look over at me. "I'm assuming you aren't now, but have you..." Ugh! This is so awkward and frustrating. I don't know how to ask without it coming out weird. I don't want to sound jealous and I don't want this to be a weird conversation, but I am curious to know if Jayce met any girls that he liked or even loved. Yes, I would love to be with him, but with my circumstances I don't think that is an option. He has a life in Oregon and I can't go back there.

I can feel Jayce watching me as I think of how to word my question. I decide just to be straightforward. "Have you been in any relationships since us?" I keep facing ahead, not wanting to see his expression from my question. A minute or so passes and he still hasn't responded. I chance a glance at him and see he's looking straight ahead. He seems uncomfortable.

Knowing I just made the evening awkward I try to fix it. "Never mind, you don't have to answer. I'm sorry I brought it up."

Jayce halts and pulls me to a stop. He walks us closer to the water, sits down in the sand and waits for me to join him. When I sit down we both look out toward the ocean as I sit there silently and wait for him to say something.

He takes a deep breath before beginning. "Yeah, I

dated a few girls. It took me a long time to start dating again, and when I did it never lasted. Evan was actually the one that talked me into starting to date again. He told me I needed to move on and that you wouldn't want me to stop living." He shrugs. "So I gave in and tried to date a few girls. Every time though I would just compare them to you. I decided after that I would just focus on college for now."

I feel Jayce's gaze on me. "Riley." He waits until I look over at him before he continues. "I'm not upset with you. It's just...after we graduated I always thought we would get engaged and then marry after college. I know that we both had to move on given the circumstances, but even when I thought you were dead I knew I wouldn't be happy with anyone else. Since I saw you on the beach the other day I wonder if I'm going to wake up and you won't really be here. Like this is all just a dream..." He shakes his head. "Anyways, what I'm trying to say is, I'm still adjusting to you really being here."

I don't really know what to say to all that so I just nod. I understand what he means though. We've always felt the same way about each other. Being with other people has never felt right to me even when I thought I would never be able to see Jayce again. Being with him now and being able to spend time with him is like a dream come true.

We both turn toward the waves and let the sound wash over us, both lost in our own thoughts.

"So do I have any competition to worry about?" Jayce teases, breaking the silence.

I roll my eyes and can't help but smile.

"I did date one guy last semester. His name is Gavin. We had class together. We only dated for about a month and we're still friends now. He and Daphne are my closest friends I have here...really, my only friends," I laugh.

"Can I ask why it didn't work out?"

I nod. "He wasn't you," I say quietly.

I feel Jayce's intense gaze on me "Riley, I..."

I look over at him to ask what he was going to say, but before I can his gaze lowers to my mouth then back up to my eyes. I begin to feel my heart rate pick up as he slowly leans in toward me. Pressing his lips on mine, we indulge in a slow and tender kiss. This kiss is different than the ones before; this kiss feels like a promise. A promise of what? I'm not sure but I hold onto it. He breaks the kiss, pulls back a little, and we hold each other's stare. Holding onto this moment, not wanting it to end. Neither of us says anything as he stands up and brushes off his pants. He pulls me up and I brush the sand off my pants too. We begin walking back toward his car in silence and I start to wonder what he was going to say.

When Jayce dropped me off at my apartment he walked me to my door and kissed me goodnight. He told me he would text me tomorrow so we could finalize the plans for tomorrow night. It seems so weird. When I left Oregon I never thought I would see him again. I don't know what will happen when he leaves, but I plan to enjoy the time I get to spend with him while I can. At some point I will probably tell my parents, but for now I don't plan on telling them any time soon. At least not until he's gone.

As I get ready for bed I think back on the evening. I feel like once we get past the hurt of me leaving and relax around each other things feel like they haven't changed between us. I wish we could pick up from the night I left his house, but the reality is we can't.

I set my alarm and climb into bed. I have to be up at eight to be to work by nine. I should've taken Spring Break off work so I could sleep in, but I could use the extra money. At least I have Friday off, which means I'll have a three-day weekend.

As I begin to doze off to sleep my phone beeps. I smile as I see Jayce's name appear on the screen. I open the text.

Jayce: *Don't worry about the storm, I'll be there to keep you warm.*
No need to check the time, you'll be forever mine.

Tears begin to prick my eyes as I read the message again. He is not making this easy for me. How am I supposed to say goodbye when he goes back to Oregon now? All night he has been saying things that hint at continuing things when he leaves, but doesn't he understand that it's not possible. I know he's probably waiting for my response.

Jayce and I had been together a few months when he sent me a sweet message that reminded me of poetry. From that night on he would send me short sweet texts before he went to sleep. I always looked forward to them. After the first week of the messages I decided to try to respond back to his with my own, so we would create our own short poem. I loved doing this with him; it was like our special thing. Sometimes they were cheesy but they were always special to me.

I feel the tears run down my cheeks as I type out a response.

Me: *If I'm always warm, and forever yours*
Hold me through the storms forever more.

I set my phone down on my nightstand and begin to sob. I don't know how long I cry for but eventually I fall asleep.

CHAPTER 12

The next morning I walk into work and I know I look horrible. Earlier when I looked in the mirror my eyes were all swollen from crying last night. The shower seemed to help a little bit, but not much. I walk toward the backroom and Sally looks up. "Oh dear, Riley. What's wrong?" I knew this was coming. I almost called in just to avoid this. Almost.

"I'm fine, Sally. I just had a rough night last night but I'm better today." I try to smile to reassure her, but she doesn't seemed convinced.

"Are you sure? We would be fine without you if you want to go home."

As good as going home and going back to bed sounds I shake my head. "I think staying would be good. It will keep my mind busy. Thank you, though."

Sally walks over and gives me a hug. "If you ever need to talk I'm here for you, dear." With that she walks out of the backroom and I put my things away and head to the front desk.

The day goes by fairly quickly. I was glad we were busy today because it kept my mind off of Jayce. The message he sent me last night made me realize that he isn't going to just let me go when he goes back to Oregon. He will fight for me; I can feel it. I shouldn't be happy about this but I am. I know I should stop this right now before it goes any further but I'm already too far in. Call me selfish, but I want to spend these last few days with him and see what happens.

I walk into our apartment and see Daphne in the kitchen cooking "Hey! I'm fixing dinner. Are you hungry?" She looks over her shoulder and smiles.

I nod, "Yeah, smells great! One of these days I'll have to return the favor for all these times you cook dinner." I hear her laugh as I walk into my room and put my things on my bed. When I walk back out Daphne is finishing up dinner, so I go grab plates out of the cupboard. We both begin fixing our food and go sit down to eat.

"So what are the plans for tonight?" I ask after a few minutes.

"I think we are going to go to the club we went to the other night. I'm not sure on the time yet. I think Ryan mentioned going around nine."

Daphne looks up from her plate and smiles really big. "So how'd your date go last night?"

"It was good. We had a good time. I'm glad I went."

She gives me an *I told you so* look and goes back to eating her food.

Once I finish I pick my plate up and rinse it off in the sink. I begin cleaning up the mess and a few minutes later Daphne helps me. We don't say much while we wash the dishes. Once everything is cleaned up I head to my room. "I'm going to go rest for a bit."

I close my door, flop down on my bed and close my eyes. I haven't been sleeping well at all lately. Hopefully things will settle down and I'll be able to get back on a normal sleeping schedule. The lack of sleep is beginning to catch up with me. I am just beginning to doze off when my phone beeps. Rolling over, I pick up my phone off the nightstand and read the text.

Jayce: *Hey! Ryan and I will be there to pick you girls up at 9. I can't wait to see you!*

I feel my mouth tug into a smile as I type out a response.

Me: *Sounds good! See you tonight! :)*

I look at the time and see I have another hour before I'll need to get ready. I set my alarm on my phone and roll back over and decide to take a short nap.

***

"Knock! Knock!"

I just finished putting my makeup on when I hear Jayce. I walk out of the bathroom and into my room to see Jayce looking around.

"I see you're already making yourself at home," I tease.

He stops and looks up from the pictures on my bulletin board and smiles. "I figured you wouldn't mind." He walks over and stops in front of me. His gaze travels from my eyes, down my body, and back up. I'm wearing dark skinny jeans, a royal blue fitted V-neck top, tall black boots, and my hair is styled in loose curls.

"Do I pass your inspection, Jayce?" I turn around in a circle for added effect.

He presses his finger to his lips as if thinking about his answer and smiles. "I think we may just want to stay in for the night."

I shake my head and laugh. "I don't think so."

"What about me?" I'm confused at first until he begins to spin around. He's wearing dark denim jeans and a charcoal button up long sleeve shirt with the sleeves rolled up. His hair looks like he just ran his hands through it after he got out of the shower and called it good. He looks hot as usual. Maybe I should consider his offer about staying here tonight. He does a full circle and stops to face me, waiting for my answer.

I shrug. "You look okay." I turn away and grab my things so he can't see my smile.

He laughs, "I think your eyes are saying something different."

Turning back to face him I roll my eyes. "I don't think I need to boost your ego any more than it already is."

He chuckles. "You were thinking about my offer to stay here, weren't you?" What is he, a mind reader?

I walk over and smile as I take his hand in mine. "I don't think so. Let's go."

With another laugh he follows me out of my room and into the family room. I don't see Daphne so she must be finishing up getting ready. Ryan is sitting on the couch and he looks up and smiles when we walk in. "Hey, Riley."

"Hey."

Noticing his other friends aren't there I look over at Jayce. "Are your other friends coming?"

"Yeah, they are going to meet us there."

Daphne emerges from her room. "All right, I'm ready to go."

After Ryan goes to her he leans in and whispers something in her ear, and Daphne giggles in response. Placing his hand on the small of her back, they begin to leave. I think Ryan may like Daphne the same way she likes him. She won't admit it to me but I know she does. From the look in Ryan's eyes when Daphne walked in and how he acted, I would say the feelings go both ways. Interesting.

I'm snapped out of my thinking when I feel Jayce come up behind me and leans down by my ear.

"Ready?" he whispers. I nod. He wraps his arm around my shoulder and we head out the door.

When we get to the car Ryan is in the driver's seat and Daphne in the passenger seat. Jayce opens the door for me and I get in, scooting over to make room for him. Once he's settled we drive to the club.

Twenty minutes later we arrive and the club is already filling up. We weave through the crowd and find a table by the dance floor. The guys ask what we want to drink and walk over to the bar. A few people are already dancing but most are hanging around the tables. Daphne and I don't really try to visit since we would have to yell to talk to each other, so we both just take in the atmosphere and listen to the music.

A few minutes later the guys walk over to us with the drinks. When they get to the table Jayce hands me my drink, sits in the seat next to me and rests his arm over the back of my chair. I know we've hung out several times already, but it still seems weird to be here with him. I glance over and see that he looks so comfortable and happy being here with me too. My lips tug up into a smile.

Jayce leans down by my ear. "What are you smiling about?"

"Just that I'm glad you're here."

He grins. "Me too." He presses a chaste kiss to my lips and I blush. I'm not used to affection in public. The only guy I've been in a relationship with besides Jayce is Gavin, and he never really kissed me in public places. We both stare at one another like we can't believe we are sitting here together.

Our moment is broken when two guys approach our table, "About time you got here," I hear Ryan say with a laugh.

One is about Jayce's height with brown hair and a five o'clock shadow look going. He laughs as he looks over at Ryan. "Yeah, well, pretty boy here," he points to the guy next to him, "took an hour to fix his hair."

I look over to "pretty boy" and the description is fitting. It seems the only thing missing is the nicely pressed suit. He is probably somewhere around six foot; his short, golden honey-colored hair is styled with gel and his face is clean-shaven. He is wearing a light blue polo shirt with dark blue jeans.

"Yeah, yeah—whatever, John. It didn't take me an hour to fix my hair." Pretty Boy laughs, whom I'm assuming is Spencer.

"Riley, Daphne. This is John," Jayce points to the first one with brown hair, "and this is Spencer. Guys, this is Riley and Daphne," he continues, pointing to each of us and we both say hi.

We all begin to visit and sip our drinks. Well, the guys visit and tell us college stories and Daph and I chime in every once in a while. I'm working on my third drink when Daphne comes around the table and looks over at Jayce. "Sorry, Jayce, I'm taking her out to dance." With that she grabs my hand and pulls me out on the dance floor.

We both begin to sway our hips to the beat of the music. We're laughing and having a good time, messing around and dancing. I look over and see Jayce watching me. We lock eyes with each other; he smiles and winks at me. I smile back at him. He turns back to his friends and laughs at something one of them says.

I know nobody is perfect, but Jayce is my perfect. There is no one else out there for me but him. I gave him my heart back in high school and he will carry it with him forever whether he wants it or not. I know it's his.

"Girl, you have it bad for him." Daphne gives me a light shove and breaks my longing stare.

"I know."

After a couple songs Jayce and Ryan walk over

toward us. Ryan goes up behind Daphne, places his hands on her hips and begins dancing with her. She looks over her shoulder and smiles coyly at him. She looks really happy with him. And she says I have it bad for Jayce? Looks like I'm not the only one. I chuckle to myself.

After several songs I move my gaze over to where Spencer and John are visiting at our table. "How come John and Spencer aren't out here?" I ask Jayce.

"They aren't much for dancing," he laughs.

We continue swaying, and I wish I could stay in Jayce's arms forever. I close my eyes and begin to memorize the feeling of his hands holding my hips. His body pressed against mine as we move to the music together. He brushes his lips against my neck and my body tingles in response.

"You wanna go sit down?" I jump as Jayce whispers in my ear.

I turn around to face him. "You need to stop coming up behind me and whispering in my ear." I try to glare at him but from the smile on his face I know I didn't succeed.

He places his hands on my hips and I jump from the contact. "Maybe you need to stop being so jumpy." He chuckles in my ear. He begins moving my hips to the music and I melt into his touch.

We decide to dance for another song then we all head back over to our table and Jayce goes up to the bar to get us drinks. When he comes back he has a mini tray of six shots. Setting the tray down, he passes everyone a shot. He holds his up and everyone follows suit. He looks directly at me as he says, "To new beginnings."

"Cheers!" we all say as we toss back the shot and set our glasses down.

Jayce grabs my hand and begins pulling me toward the patio door. We make it out the door and I begin to giggle. Jayce walks us over to a table and places me in a seat, which makes my giggles turn to laughter. Jayce stands between my legs and looks at me with amusement. "I love the sound of your laugh." He reaches up and tucks a stray hair behind my ear. "What are you laughing about?"

Apparently the alcohol is taking effect. I don't usually drink that often except for over break, so it doesn't take much for me. I shake my head and laugh harder. After a few moments I wipe the tears that have leaked from laughing and look up at Jayce. "I'm not really sure," I gasp.

His brows furrow in confusion. I place my hands on his cheeks and brush my thumbs across his brows. "I've missed you," I whisper as I pull his forehead to mine.

He smiles. "I've missed you too."

He places his hands on my wrists, pulls them down from his face and intertwines our fingers. "I don't think you needed that last shot," he chuckles.

I lean forward and place my forehead against his shoulder. "Probably not," I mumble. I can feel his shoulders vibrate as he laughs.

"I'll go get you a water, okay?" I sit up and nod.

"I'll be right back." He turns to the door that leads inside.

I sit back in the chair and lean my head against the wall as I close my eyes. A few moments later I feel a chill run up my spine as I get the feeling of being watched again. It's not the good chills either. I feel myself instantly sober up. I open my eyes and glance around. About six other people are out here on the patio and they all seem to be minding their own business. I look out at the street, and other than a few empty parked cars I don't see anything. I can feel my heart rate and breathing pick up as I continue searching. It has been a few days since I had this sensation and I just assumed maybe I was imagining things, but now the feeling is back and I don't like it. I don't feel like I'm safe, and start to wonder if it has anything to do with Frank.

I startle as Jayce sets my water down on the table in front of me. Maybe Jayce is right about me being jumpy.

Jayce steps in front of me and grabs my hands. "Hey. Are you okay?" He looks me over with worry.

I nod, grab my water, and take a drink. Closing my eyes I let the cold water run through me. I look up at Jayce. "I'm ready to go. Can you take me home?"

He studies me for a moment and then nods, "Okay, I'll text the guys and let them know." A quick text later he takes my hand. "Let's go."

CHAPTER 13

In the car Jayce and I are both silent. I lean my head against the window and close my eyes. The whole way home I keep wondering if I really am being watched. If I am I should probably tell our marshal, but that means relocation and maybe even a new identity. Of course I don't even have proof someone is watching me; it's just a feeling. Every time I've looked around I've never seen anyone so maybe I'm just imagining things. Call it stupidity, but for now I'm not going to say anything.

Jayce parks the car at my apartment and I notice neither of us have made a move to get out. I look over and see Jayce watching me with concern. "Riley, what happened when I went to go get your water? When I left you were smiling and giggling, but then when I got back you looked really pale and scared. Almost like you were going to have a panic attack."

I decide to evade the question and ask one of my own. I meet his gaze. "Jayce, will you stay here with me tonight?" I ask quietly. I really don't want to be alone tonight. I don't feel safe and I want to feel secure again. Being in Jayce's arms does that.

He turns his body to face me. "Riley, I don't know if that's a good idea."

He's probably thinking the alcohol is talking but it's not. I really want him to stay. I need him to stay. I grab his hand. "Please, Jayce." He hesitates so I add, "I'm not expecting anything. I just want you to stay here."

He searches my eyes for a moment then nods. "Okay." He turns and gets out of the car. I watch as he mumbles to himself while he walks around to my side to open the door.

We walk silently up the stairs to my apartment. Once inside I get two waters out of the fridge and hand one to Jayce.

"Thanks."

A few sips of water later Jayce follows me to my bedroom where I get a t-shirt and a pair of cotton shorts to change into. Jayce is leaning against the doorframe watching me. I can tell he is still hesitant to stay here; not that he doesn't want to, but he's unsure about my reasons for wanting him here. I decide I need to tell him what happened tonight, so maybe he'll relax a little bit.

I sit down, and begin. "Jayce, do you remember the other day when I told you I felt like I was being watched?" He walks over to sit next to me on the bed and nods. "Well, I didn't think much of it after that, so I figured maybe I was just imagining things. When you went in to get water for me I felt it again. I looked around and couldn't see anyone that looked suspicious or anything." Jayce looks more concerned as I continue on. "I don't feel safe, Jayce." I add quietly and look away.

"Can you tell someone about it? Like the police?"

"I could tell the marshal but I don't have any proof. I haven't seen anyone suspicious, so I don't have anything to tell them." I let out a shaky breath. "Plus, I risk getting moved away again," I whisper.

Jayce begins to pace in front of me. "Riley, you need to tell someone. Your life could be in danger. What if it's the guy that they haven't found yet?"

"You think I don't know that?" I snap, feeling defensive. "I've had to live the last two and a half years like this. But I finally have a life here now and I'm not going to get it taken away again because of a few feelings that I've had. Until I have proof I'm not saying anything. It could be nothing." I know Jayce is just trying to look out for me and is concerned for my safety, but I meant what I said about not being sent away again.

Jayce stops pacing and looks at me. "Riley, you just told me you didn't feel safe."

"Yeah, well, I haven't felt safe over the last couple years, so really it's not any different," I sigh. I pick up my change of clothes off the bed and get up to head for the bathroom, but Jayce stops me.

"Look, I'm sorry. I'm not trying to tell you what to do. I just..." He looks away for a moment before locking eyes with me again. "I don't want anything to happen to you."

I nod and smile weakly at him. "I know." With that I go into the bathroom and go through my bedtime routine.

When I walk out of the bathroom I'm surprised to see that Jayce made a bed for himself on the floor next to my bed. "What are you doing?" I look from him to the blankets on the floor again.

He looks up from finishing his "bed" and smiles sheepishly. "I hope you don't mind. I grabbed some blankets from your closet." Although this isn't what I had in mind it's probably best if he sleeps on the floor. I walk over to my bed and begin to pull down the comforter. "No, that's fine. I'm sorry. I should've done that before I went into the bathroom."

"That's okay."

"You're welcome to use my bathroom to get ready

for bed if you want. I have some extra toothbrushes in the first drawer on your right if you want one." He nods and goes into the bathroom.

I crawl into my bed and snuggle down into the covers. Just as I'm beginning to doze off Jayce walks back out wearing his jeans and a plain white t-shirt. I inwardly sigh. He always looks so good in anything he wears. He chuckles as he sets his folded shirt next to his bed. Apparently I sighed out loud and he caught me checking him out.

He begins to unbutton his pants and I start to panic a little. I meant what I said when I told him I didn't expect anything. "Jayce, what are you doing?"

"I was going to sleep in my boxers and t-shirt." He looks over at me and I'm not sure what expression he sees on my face. I'm feeling a little shocked because I guess I didn't think about what he would be wearing to bed. He laughs a little as he continues "Is that going to bother you? Jeans aren't very comfortable to sleep in."

"Um, yeah, that's fine." Yeah, it's definitely a good thing he is sleeping on the floor. I roll over to face away from him and snuggle down farther in my covers. I hear as he moves around and try to tune him out. Eventually he turns off the light and I hear him lie down on the floor.

We both lay there quietly. After a while I finally break the silence. "Thank you for staying with me, Jayce." I take in a breath. "Tonight freaked me out a little bit and I didn't want to be alone." I say quietly. It's weird how in the dark it's a lot easier to say things. I feel like since he can't see me then I don't feel so vulnerable.

"You're welcome." Silence surrounds us again.

I don't know how much time passes before Jayce breaks it. "Riley, will you tell me if this happens again?" I know he's referring to being watched.

I know I can trust him so I respond without

hesitation. "Yes."

I hear him shift around for a minute, probably trying to get comfortable. "Goodnight, Elle," he says quietly.

"Goodnight, Jayce." I smile as I realize he called me Elle. He was the only one that ever called me that. It was the nickname he had given me back when we were together and I always loved when he called me that. Instead of calling me sweetheart, babe, or anything like that he would call me Elle. It was my special name. With a smile on my face I fall asleep.

***

"No!" I scream. I feel someone grab my wrist and I begin to panic. My breathing becomes faster and I try to get away. "No! Please let me go!" I need to get away. I can't let him take me away again. If he does take me I know he'll kill me this time. Strong arms wrap around my waist and pull me back. I try to get away but I'm trapped. My breaths come shorter and feel like I'm going to pass out. I'm about to give up when one word stops me short.

"Elle."

Jayce. He's here. Wait. He needs to go because otherwise he'll be in danger too.

"Elle! Wake up!" I feel hands run down the side of my face as my eyes begin to blink open. "It's just a dream, Elle. You're safe. I have you!" My eyes focus and I take in my surroundings. I look up and see a very worried Jayce looking at me. A hard body pressed up against my back. I must have a confused look on my face because he clarifies, "You were screaming and yelling. You must've had a bad dream." I sit up and look around and see that I am in my bed, and it's just me and Jayce. I lay back down and sigh. Another nightmare. I haven't had one for a while now.

"Are you okay? Do you want to talk about it?" he asks quietly.

I snuggle back into him, grab his arm and wrap it around my waist. Jayce doesn't hesitate and pulls me back closer to him and holds me tightly. I'm safe. Jayce will keep me safe. I wipe my hands across my face and realize that I must've been crying in my dream because my cheeks are damp. Taking a few deep breaths I try to calm my racing heart down.

"When we first moved here I had nightmares pretty much every night. They were always similar. The guy would come after me and try to hurt me or go after my family and friends. I went to counseling for a while and it seemed to help some. The counselor suggested I find something to help get my emotions out so I began taking kickboxing. I eventually quit counseling but I still do the kickboxing. The nightmares still come occasionally but not as often." Jayce intertwines our hands. "Tonight at the club must've triggered my nightmare." He tightens his arms around me and I hold onto the feeling of being wrapped in his embrace again. "I'll be okay," I whisper.

After a few moments I feel Jayce shift and I begin to panic a little, thinking he's going to move back down to the floor. "Jayce."

He leans up on his elbow and hovers over me. "Yeah?"

I look up into his eyes and hesitate a beat. "Will you stay up here with me?"

With the moonlight shining into the window I can see his smile. "Yeah, I'll stay with you." He leans down and places a tender kiss on my lips, then pulls back. "Goodnight, Elle" he whispers and lays back down. I probably should remind him that he won't be able to call me Elle but for now I just enjoy it.

"Goodnight, Jayce." I snuggle back farther into

him.

"Riley, I only have so much control," he growls. I chuckle as I snuggle back a little farther just to drive him crazy.

I feel him shift again. "You are being cruel," he mumbles, which only makes me smile more.

"Sorry, I'll be nice," I sigh. I start to move away but Jayce tightens his arms. Neither of us say anything and after a while I feel myself drifting off to sleep. Just before I doze off to sleep I feel Jayce nuzzle into my neck and feel a feather-like kiss. With that I fall into the best sleep I've had in almost three years.

CHAPTER 14

I begin to stir awake but realize I can't move very much. I feel arms tighten around my waist and for a minute I begin to panic. I feel trapped, and I hate that sensation. "It's just me, Elle," Jayce whispers in my ear. I immediately relax and remember the events that happened last night.

He props up on his elbow and looks down at me and smiles. "Did you sleep okay?"

I nod and smile back at him, then get up to go use the bathroom and brush my teeth. "I'll be right back," I say over my shoulder. I go into the bathroom and make myself presentable. When I walk back in Jayce is lying on his back with his hands behind his head. I lean against the doorframe and watch him. He is staring up at the ceiling and his brows are furrowed in deep thought. After a few minutes I slowly approach the bed and make it to the foot before Jayce notices me and he smiles. He pats the spot next to him. "Come here."

He pulls the covers back and holds them up for me. I crawl up the bed and lay down next to him and he pulls me up so my head is laying on his chest. He wraps the covers back around us and begins rubbing my back.

"Jayce, what were you thinking about when I came in?" I begin drawing designs with my fingers on his chest mindlessly.

"Just thinking…" I lay there silently, waiting for him to go on. He hesitates before he continues. "See, right now while I'm here I can know that you're safe. But when I go back to Oregon I'll be wondering if you're okay."

"I'll be safe, Jayce. I'll just be more careful going places." I smile up at him to try to assure him, but he doesn't look like he's convinced. "I'll be fine. You don't need to worry." I can see he wants to argue but he lets it go and nods. I lay my head back down on his chest. Neither of us has directly asked the question about what will happen when he does go back. I think we are afraid of the answer and at the same time don't really know. I gave him my number, which I should've never done. If his phone is being monitored or tracked that could lead Frank to me. But I decided to take that risk anyway. But once he goes back I don't know if we should continue to keep in touch. I know it would be mean, but I could get my number changed without him knowing. I feel myself tense up. Just saying it makes me want to cry. I don't think I could hurt him a second time. Not that the first time was really my fault.

"Hey," Jayce whispers. I look up at him. "What's going on in that head of yours?"

Before I can respond there is a knock on my door. "Riley?" Saved by Daphne.

"Yeah?"

"Ryan and I are going to go to the beach today with Spencer and John. Do you guys want to go?"

I look over at Jayce, silently asking him, and he shrugs. "Yeah, we'll go. What time are you guys leaving?"

"Probably thirty minutes."

"Okay." Once I hear her walk away I look back at Jayce and grin. "Well, looks like we should get up and get ready." I start to rise but don't get far. I laugh as he wraps his arms around my waist and pulls me back down against him. "We're not done talking about this. I know that whatever it is, it's bothering you, and we don't have time to talk about it now. But we will later."

"Okay," I smile. I know we will have to have this conversation at some point, so there is no use trying to ignore it. But like he said we don't have time to talk about it now, which is fine with me because I wasn't ready to.

He smiles back. "Good. Now let's get ready to go."

***

Thirty minutes later Jayce and I are in my car heading toward his place so he can get his trunks. Daphne and Ryan took the guys' car and went ahead to the beach to meet up with Spencer and John. The house that the guys are staying in is right on the beach, but they wanted to go to the area closer to the boardwalk.

We don't talk much on the way. Once we get to the beach I notice it's pretty busy with people probably taking advantage of their last few days of Spring Break. Jayce and I get out of the car and I get my bag out of the backseat. We begin walking toward where Daphne said to meet and Jayce reaches down to grab my hand and intertwines our fingers.

"Riley! Over here!" I look over to the direction of the voice and see Daphne waving like a crazy person. Jayce and I laugh as we head over to where she is. When we get there I drop my bag by her towel that is already laid out.

"You do realize that you looked like a crazy

person jumping up and down, right?"

She laughs. "Yeah, I know, and now you're sitting with the crazy person."

I shake my head and laugh as I reach into my bag, pulling out two beach towels and laying them out by Daphne's. Daphne looks over at Jayce. "The guys went over there," she points over to the opposite direction we just came from, "to play some volleyball." Jayce nods and goes over with the other guys.

Once he is out of earshot she starts on me. "So...you and Jayce, huh?" She wags her eyebrows.

I roll my eyes. "It's not what you think. He stayed last night but nothing happened." I sit down on my towel and lean back on my hands. Daphne sits next to me on her towel and mimics my position.

"But you want to?" she asks as she glances over at me.

I sigh. "We are not having this discussion."

She laughs, "All right, all right. I already know the answer anyway. It's written all over your face."

I snort. "Whatever."

We both look over toward the boys and watch as they toss the ball back and forth over the net. They all took their shirts off since the temperature warmed up a bit. I can't help but watch Jayce's muscles flex as he jumps up to hit the ball. He definitely got more muscle over the past couple years. I glance at Daphne and notice that she's watching Ryan like I was watching Jayce.

"So...you and Ryan?" I say, mocking her.

She looks over at me. "What about me and Ryan?" she asks innocently.

I shake my head. "I see how it is. You want all the information about Jayce and me, but want to play dumb when I turn the table around?"

She laughs and looks over at the boys again. "I don't know, honestly. Like I said before, once he leaves we'll probably go back to our own lives. I mean we talk, hang out, and we've kissed several times..." She shrugs. "But we haven't really talked about what happens when he leaves."

"What do you want?"

"I like him and I feel like there is a connection with him. But it doesn't matter because he'll be leaving and then I'm sure he'll forget all about me." She turns away and looks out at the ocean.

"Have you tried to talk to him about it? I mean, maybe he feels the same about you but doesn't want to freak you out." I know I pretty much told her to stay out of the things that involved Jayce and me, but things between us are more complicated. I mean, I have someone after me, and the more people I have involved in my life the more people I put at risk. But she and Ryan only have about a month and a half left of school and then they could spend the summer figuring things out. At least one of us should be happy and end up with the person they like.

"I'm not going to be the one to say anything. Like I told you before I don't like to complicate things. We are both enjoying the time together and I don't want to try to make things difficult. I'll be fine." She smiles sadly.

I nod, knowing that she doesn't want to continue the conversation. After a while Daphne and I turn over and lie on our stomachs. We are both lying in silence with our eyes closed. I lay there listening to the waves as they wash up on the shore.

"Ryan!" I look over and see Ryan lifting Daphne over his shoulders. He begins running toward the water with Daphne kicking and smacking him on the back, which doesn't seem to faze him as he continues sprinting. I laugh as I hear her yelling at him to put her down and how ridiculous she looks. He reaches the water and continues until it is up almost to his waist. Then he cradles Daphne and tosses her into the water as she screams. When she comes up for air she spits out the water and wipes her face. "Ryan! I will get you back for that!" Then she begins running toward him while he just stands there laughing.

Next thing I know I'm being lifted up in the air and thrown over Jayce's shoulder.

"Jayce! You put me down!"

He continues toward the water. "I don't think so," he laughs.

"Please, Jayce! The water is probably freezing."

"I know you've been in colder water than this, Riley." he chuckles.

He reaches the water and I bring my hands up and begin to tickle him. He squirms away while still trying to walk deeper into the water. "Riley, you're going to make me drop you if you don't stop," He warns, trying not to laugh.

"You're going to drop me anyway," I say as I continue to tickle him.

He pulls me back over his shoulder and cradles me in his arms and I begin to feel the water brush against my back. I squeal and try arch away from the water, but fail as I feel it soak my backside.

"Jayce Aaron Cooper! Put me down now!" Right after the words leave my mouth I know exactly what he is going to do.

He flashes a mischievous smile. "Okay." Before I can respond he tosses me into the water. When I go under I gasp from the shock of the cold. I feel like I am being poked with tiny needles all over my body and when I gasp I inhale a bunch of water. My nose and lungs begin to burn. I push off the bottom, reach the surface, and begin coughing to get the water out. Jayce runs over to me. "Are you okay?" I look up and can tell he doesn't know if he should laugh or feel bad.

I glare at him and begin walking back toward

shore. Once I get past him I turn and tackle him into the water. He isn't expecting it so he goes down into the water with me. When we both surface he is the one coughing now. I didn't actually think he would go under, and by the expression on his face he didn't expect me to tackle him either. I burst out laughing and Jayce locks eyes with me. "You think this is funny?" I nod and continue laughing. He begins to stalk over to me like I'm his prey. He stops right in front of me and leans down closer to my face. "You think it's funny that you tackled me into the water?" I see his lips twitch, showing that he is trying not to laugh.

I nod and smile sweetly at him. "Yep."

He wraps his arms around my waist and pulls me close to him, and I gasp in surprise. He leans down and I think that he is going to kiss me. I begin to melt into him but right before his lips brush against mine he lifts me up and tosses me back into the water. Right before I hit I hear him laughing.

When I reach the surface coughing again, I peer through stringy wet tendrils of hair and see Jayce still laughing. When he sees that I surfaced he walks over chuckling. "Sorry Riley, it was too easy." He stops in front of me and I try to glare at him, but I'm not even mad at him. The water is freezing, but I'm having such a good time with him that I don't even care about the temperature. I approach him, and I can see him watching me closely, wondering what I'm going to do. I continue to glare at him as I stop in front of him. "Riley?" Jayce says hesitantly. He looks so unsure what to do or say that I finally crack and begin laughing. The look on his face only makes me laugh harder. I glance up and see that he is confused, but eventually he joins in and laughs with me.

Once I calm down I walk up and wrap my arms around his neck. He looks down at me and smiles.

"You're not going to get me back?"

I laugh and shake my head. I gently pull his face down to mine. I place a soft kiss on his lips and pull back and smile. "But next time you might not get off the hook so easy," I tease. He chuckles as he steps back and takes my hand. I realize as we walk back to our spot that I said next time. Knowing that the week is coming to an end I know we won't have that many "next times", which makes me sad to think about.

I look over where Daphne and the guys are and see they are all sitting around talking and laughing. From the looks of it Daphne must've forgiven Ryan for tossing her in the water too, but not before she got her revenge. They are both wrapped up in towels sitting side by side. Jayce follows my gaze and laughs, "Looks like Daphne got Ryan back."

"So whose idea was it to throw us in the water?"

He grins proudly. "Mine."

"Of course it was," I say dryly.

When we make it to our spot John looks up and laughs. "I can't believe you and Ryan both got tackled by these two." He points to Daphne and me. "Looks like your plan backfired."

"Shut up, John," Ryan says. "She caught me off guard."

John nods. "Yeah, whatever you say." He laughs and we all join in. Jayce and I sit on our towels and I lie down on my back, hoping the sun will help dry my suit faster. As I lie there I close my eyes and just listen to the guys talk and laugh. It's funny how even though most of us have just met it feels like we have all been friends for a long time. We are all so comfortable around each other. John and Spencer don't seem bothered to have Daphne and me around at all. Too bad in two days the guys will be going back to their lives in Oregon and Daphne and I will go back to our lives here.

At four o'clock we all decide to head back to our

places to shower and relax for a while. The guys invited us over to their place for the night. Ryan's parents' house has a heated pool, hot tub, and a game room, so we are going to hang out there and order pizza.

Jayce walks with me to the parking lot and Daphne and Ryan follow a little behind. We get to my car and I open the door to the backseat and toss my bag in. I shut the door and turn to face Jayce. He places his hands on my waist and pulls me close to him and my hands go up to his chest. I feel him hesitate a moment before he speaks. "Riley, I want you to stay at our place tonight." I pull back a little but Jayce holds me in place. I start to say something but Jayce goes on. "I want to know that you're safe, and having you with me I'll know that."

I sigh, "Jayce, I don't need a babysitter…"

He cuts me off before I can continue and smiles at me. "Good, because I don't want to be your babysitter. I know you can take care of yourself. I don't just want you to stay so I know you're safe. I want you to stay so I can be with you." I want to stay with him too, but I don't know if that is a good idea. I know he stayed last night, but I was freaked out and asked him because I really didn't want to be alone. He's going to be leaving in a couple of days and I really should start putting distance between us so it won't be as hard when he leaves. Who am I kidding though? I'm already attached and know that I will be heartbroken again when he has to leave.

He can see that I'm debating, so he leans down and brushes his lips against mine. "Please, Riley." He pulls back a little and smiles. Well, how can I say no to him now?

I roll my eyes at him and can't help but smile. "Fine."

He places a kiss on my forehead. "Good, I'll see you tonight."

CHAPTER 15

When Daphne and I get back to our apartment, we both shower. Once I'm dressed I go into my room and walk to my closet. I pull out a bag and begin packing for an overnight with Jayce. Once I have everything I need I walk to the kitchen and get a water out of the fridge, then go sit on the couch next to Daphne.

"So Jayce asked me to stay over tonight."

Daphne turns down the TV and looks over at me. "And what did you say?"

"I'm going to stay."

"That's exciting," she squeals.

I nod. "Are you staying tonight too?"

She shrugs. "I don't know. I mean, Ryan told me I could but I don't know if it's a good idea. I told him I would think about it." She sighs and leans back against the couch. "I'm just going to see how the night goes, I guess."

"That makes sense." I lean back against the couch with her. We sit there in silence for a while, both lost in thought.

"So have you heard from Gavin since he's been

gone?" Daphne asks.

"Yeah, he actually texted me today. He said he gets back on Sunday, and asked if we wanted to meet him and Matt for lunch sometime next week."

"That sounds great. It will be good to hang out with the locals again." She smiles. I can tell she's not looking forward to this week ending either but I don't say anything.

"What time do the guys want us to come over?" Daphne asks.

"I think they said they were going to order the pizza around seven, so we should be there around then." She nods, unmutes the TV, and then we zone for the next hour until it's time to go.

***

When we pull into the driveway of the house Daphne and I stare in amazement. The house is beautiful. Jayce and I stopped by earlier but I didn't get a chance to actually look since we were in a hurry. It is a gray two-story house with white shutters by all the windows. It has a white deck that appears to wrap all the way around the house. Off two of the upstairs rooms there are large windows with small balconies.

Daphne looks over at me once we are parked, "This house is gorgeous! The inside is beautiful too." We both look back to the house.

"Yeah, it is. I didn't get a chance to see the inside yet, but I'm sure it is," I say. We both open our doors and begin to get out.

"Hey!" I look up and see Jayce walking down the steps to us.

I step out of the car and grab my bag, then turn to him and smile, "Hey!"

He walks over and wraps his arms around my waist. "I'm glad you're here."

I roll my eyes playfully. "You've seen me pretty

much all day. Aren't you tired of me yet?" I tease.

He grins. "Never. Let's go inside. Pizza should be here anytime." Daphne and I follow Jayce up the steps to the house. When we get to the door Ryan opens it. "Hey! You guys made it!" He steps aside and lets us through.

"Welcome to my humble abode." Ryan gestures around the entryway. The inside of the house is just as beautiful as the outside. I couldn't even imagine living in a house like this. Growing up we weren't poor, but we weren't rich either. We always had the things we needed, and I was able to do some things I wanted to do. I guess you could say we were considered middle class. My group of friends grew up the same way I did, so seeing a house like this is completely new to me.

Jayce grabs my hand. "Here. We can take your stuff up to my room, and then I can give you a tour of the place." I nod and follow him. I glance over my shoulder and see Daphne following Ryan down the hall.

When we get to the top of the stairs we turn right. "The master bedroom is down on the main floor, which is where Ryan is staying. Then there are four bedrooms upstairs and two bathrooms. Spencer and John's rooms are back that way." He points in the opposite direction. We come to a stop in front of a room. "And this is the room we'll be staying in." He winks and opens the door.

I walk past him as I feel my cheeks blush. I don't want him to see that I'm a little nervous. I know he stayed with me last night, but I was freaked out and didn't really think too much about it then. But tonight I'm not sure what will happen. I haven't been with anyone since Jayce. He was the first and only and that was over two and a half years ago.

Jayce walks up behind me and I startle. "Relax, Riley." He turns me around so I'm facing him, then he lifts my chin up gently so I'm looking into his eyes. "Just like you told me last night I'm not expecting anything. I just want to be with you. I don't care if we just sleep, or talk all night, or whatever. I just want you here with me. Okay?" He smiles sweetly at me. This is Jayce. I've always felt comfortable around him and never felt nervous. He's still the same sweet Jayce I knew back then. I look into his eyes and see the love shining there, and the nervousness fades away.

I smile up at him. "Okay."

He lets me go and walks over to the bed and sets my bag down. He points toward a door. "That's the bathroom. We'll have it to ourselves so you don't need to worry about the other guys." I nod and see a door that looks like it leads outside.

"Where does that go?" I point to the door.

"Come on, I'll show you." We walk out the door and I gasp. It leads to a small balcony that overlooks the beach and the view is breathtaking. Jayce grabs my hand and walks me out to the railing. I look out onto the beach and watch for a few moments as the waves crash onto the shore. I close my eyes and listen to the sound. I would love to live on the beach and be able to just come out and listen to the ocean all the time.

I sigh and turn to look at Jayce. "This is beautiful."

"Yeah, it's pretty awesome. I wouldn't mind staying here," he chuckles.

"Look down there." He points below us. I look and see the kidney-shaped swimming pool and off to the side a large hot tub. "The pool is heated so we'll be able to go swimming tonight if you want to."

"Sounds good."

"We should probably head back downstairs. The food is probably here." We both turn and walk back inside.

When we get down to the kitchen everyone is already grabbing plates and their food. We walk over to the counter and Jayce hands me a plate. "Thanks." We slide over to the boxes of pizza and I take a couple slices. Jayce puts a few slices on his plates and then walks over to the fridge. "You want something to drink?"

I nod. "Yeah, I'll have a water." He grabs a bottle and hands it to me, then gets one for himself. We walk outside to sit on the patio with everyone else and I sit across from Daphne and Jayce sits down on the other side of me across from Ryan.

As we eat we all visit, joke around, and laugh. I never would've guessed this was how I would be spending my Spring Break. I figured Daphne would be dragging me out every night and we would be spending the days at the beach. Who would've thought that Jayce would end up here and we would run into each other? I glance at Ryan and Daphne. They really are good together. I've seen a change in her this week, a good change, and I know it's because of Ryan. It's too bad he lives on the other side of the country.

Spencer and John both seem like good guys. They always give each other a hard time but in a joking way. Spencer is known as the pretty boy and John reminds me of the bad boy type. They are all fun to be around. It sucks that they have to go back.

"Are you ready to go swimming?" Jayce asks.

"Yeah."

I get up and grab my trash and go throw it away. When I return I see Jayce laughing at something Ryan says and when he sees me his grin gets bigger. He says something to Ryan, walks over to me and intertwines our hands together. "Let's go get our suits on." I follow him toward the house.

When we get to his room he shuts the door and turns toward me. "You can go ahead and change in the bathroom first." I nod and get my suit. In the bathroom I pull on a pair of cotton shorts and a tank over my suit and walk back into the bedroom. Jayce is already changed into his board shorts. His gaze travels down my body and back up and he grins. "You know what? I don't think I'm feeling very good all of a sudden. Maybe we should just hang out in here and watch movies." He winks.

I roll my eyes and put my other clothes in my bag. "Your lame attempts to get me to stay in here aren't going to work." I turn my face to hide my smile. "And you think Ryan's pick-up lines are bad."

He chuckles as he walks over to me. I feel him stop behind me as I zip up my bag and he wraps his arms around my waist. He leans down by my ear. "I might not get you to stay in here right now, but later...." He trails off as his lips brush my ear and I shiver. He chuckles as he pulls back and walks over to the door. He turns around to look at me. "Ready to go?" He smiles innocently.

I grab the towels off the bed and walk over to him. I let it go for now and decide to get him back later. "Yep"

He opens the door and we head out to the pool. When we get there Spencer and John are the only ones out there. I walk over to the tables and chairs and set the towels down. Spencer and John are sitting at the table drinking a beer. Jayce walks over to the ledge and glances around the pool. I walk up behind him and grab on to his hand. "Is the water warm?" I ask curiously.

"It should be. Are you going to get in?"

I smile sweetly at him. "Yeah, are you?"

"Yeah, you want to jump in with me?"

"Sure." I walk back over to our stuff. I glance over where Spencer and John were sitting and notice them getting up to go get another beer. With no one around I take advantage of the opportunity. Jayce wants to tease me? Well, it's only fair I return the favor. I begin to take my shorts and tank off and notice Jayce watching me. I set my clothes on the table and walk over to him. "Are you ready?" I look up at him and smile innocently. I can see the desire in his eyes, and am happy to know that I have the same effect on him.

He shakes his head lightly. "Um, yeah." I walk over to the deep end and stand on the ledge. Jayce comes up next to me. He looks out over the water, and I decide this is my chance to get him back for earlier at the beach.

I place my hand on his lower back. "Hey, Jayce." He looks over at me and I feel a grin spread across my face, knowing he won't see this coming. "There's something I want to do."

His eyes begin to search mine. "What?"

"This!" I say as I push him into the pool.

"That was so hilarious!" I turn around and see everyone burst out laughing. I didn't even notice them come back out. "Did you see his face when you pushed him in?" John hoots.

I turn back around when I hear Jayce surface the water. He wipes the drops from his face and turns to look right at me. He narrows his eyes. "Riley! I will get you back for that!" I see his lips twitch as if fighting off a laugh.

I shrug. "I was just getting you back for earlier at the beach."

"You already got me back for that when you tackled me. We were even." He begins to swim toward the edge of the pool. "But now..." He hops out and begins to stalk over to me.

"Jayce, you should've seen your expression, man! I wish I would've recorded that!" Ryan laughs.

"Shut up, Ryan!" He begins to walk faster toward me and I turn to run. "Just get your camera ready for when I get Riley back now." Then he takes off running after me. I speed out toward the lawn but I'm not fast enough because next thing I know I'm slung over Jayce's shoulders. I don't even try to fight him because I won't win anyway.

"You're not even going to try to fight me this time?" He laughs. "You're making this too easy."

"There's no point," I retort.

We make it back to the edge of the pool and Jayce flips me back over his shoulder. He places me on the ground but keeps his arms wrapped tightly around my waist so I can't escape. "Now we are going to jump in together like we originally discussed, and you aren't getting out of it this time." He smirks down at me.

I laugh as he lifts me up so I'm eye level with him. "Are you ready?"

Before I can respond he jumps into the pool with me in his arms.

CHAPTER 16

We end up swimming for a couple of hours. After Jayce and I jumped in everyone else joined us. We played a couple games of volleyball with no net and then just messed around in the pool. I climb out of the pool behind Jayce. He grabs our towels and hands one to me.

"Thanks."

"Hey, Jayce! Come here," Ryan calls over.

I wrap my towel around myself, then grab my clothes off the table. I turn around and see Ryan and Jayce having a private conversation. Jayce looks upset, and Ryan looks at him sadly and says something else. Jayce nods and walks back over to me. When he looks up and sees me watching him he smiles but it seems forced. Something isn't right. Whatever Ryan told Jayce he isn't happy about.

"Everything okay?" I ask when he stops in front of me.

"Yeah, let's go get changed." He grabs my hand and we walk up to his room.

Once we're alone I grab a change of clothes.

When I turn around I see Jayce leaning against the closed door with his arms crossed, watching me. I set my clothes back on the bed and walk over to him. Placing my hands on his chest, I catch his gaze. "Jayce? What's wrong?"

He slowly brings his hands up and cups my face, then leans down and gives me a tender kiss. When he pulls back he smiles. "I'm glad you're staying here tonight." He's avoiding the question, but in this moment I don't care anymore. I know that when he goes back to Oregon I will be completely heartbroken. I love him and I've never stopped. I need to tell him how I feel, and I want to show him. I may never get to see or talk to him again and I don't want any regrets.

"Jayce." I look into his eyes and see his love.

"I love you." His eyes widen a little from shock and I can tell he wasn't expecting me to say that. "I never stopped loving you. I know you have to go back to Oregon, but I can't have you leave without..." He cuts me off with a kiss. The kiss is full of love, desire, and then turns to hunger. He wraps his arms around my waist and pulls me closer. After a few moments he pulls back and leans his forehead against mine. We are both breathing heavily as we try to catch our breath.

"Riley." He pauses until our eyes meet. "No one else makes me feel the way you do. I've always felt that what we had was special. I know I have to go back to Oregon..." He glances away for a moment like he is hiding something, but I'm too caught up in the moment to worry about it. "But Riley, I will find a way for us to be together. I love you." He brushes his lips against mine. "I won't lose you again. Okay?" I nod and it's then I realize I have tears streaming down my face. Jayce reaches up and brushes them away with his thumbs and murmurs, "I've always loved you, Riley."

"Show me," I whisper. Stunned, he pulls back a little and searches my face. "Jayce, I want to—"

He interrupts. "Are you sure? We don't have to do anything, Riley."

I cup his face in my hands and pull it down to mine. I brush my lips against his in a soft kiss and whisper, "Yes."

He crushes his mouth to mine as he lifts me up and carries me over to the bed.

***

A while later Jayce and I lay on his bed intertwined together under the sheets. Jayce lightly skims his hand down my back and I laugh and arch away from his touch. "Jayce!"

"You always were really ticklish," he laughs. He reaches back to do it again. I try to move away from him, but he wraps his arms around my waist and pulls me back against him. "Where do you think you're going?"

"Away from you if you keep tickling me." I narrow my eyes at him.

"Okay. Okay, I'll stop." He holds his hands up in surrender.

"Good." I lay my head back on his chest and snuggle back into his side as he wraps his arm around me. He grabs a piece of my hair and begins to twirl it around his finger, "I don't think I told you yet but I do like this new hair color on you." I smile against his chest as he continues to play with my hair, "I miss your honey blonde but this color suites you too." I close my eyes as his fingers massage over my head.

"Can we stay here forever?" I sigh.

I feel Jayce's chest vibrate as he chuckles. "If it were possible, I would." He places a kiss on top of my head.

My phone begins to vibrate, informing me of a text. I roll out of bed, wrap a sheet around me, and walk over to Jayce's dresser. I pick up my phone and look down at the screen. It's a message from Daphne.

Daphne: *Just wanted to let you know I'm not staying here tonight. I can come back in the morning and get you if you need me to.*

I stare down at my phone, confused why Daphne all of sudden decided to not stay. She told me while we were swimming that she was staying.

Me: *Did something happen? Is everything okay?*

Daphne: *Yeah, everything is fine, but they are leaving tomorrow. So I don't see a point in staying.*

Tomorrow? Tomorrow is Saturday and Jayce said they weren't leaving till Sunday. He never told me. Why wouldn't he tell me?

Me: *Don't leave yet.*

"Everything okay?"

I look up from my phone and narrow my eyes. "*Is* everything okay, Jayce?"

He sits up in the bed and looks at me confused. "What do you mean, Riley?"

"I thought you were leaving Sunday. Why didn't you tell me you were leaving tomorrow?"

"I was going to—" He begins to get off the bed to come over to me but I hold up my hand.

"Don't!" I walk over to my bag and grab my clothes. I begin putting them on fast and throw the rest in my bag. "Riley, why are you getting so upset about this? I just found out tonight. I was going to tell you..."

"Yeah? When? After we slept together?" I snap.

He looks taken aback. "Riley, it wasn't like that and you know it. I was going to tell you when we got up here but then I didn't get the chance to. Plus it's not like you didn't know I was going to be leaving. It's just a day sooner than we thought. Ryan told me tonight that his parents need us to leave tomorrow because the house has to be cleaned Sunday before some other renters get here." He stands up and wraps the sheet around his waist and slowly moves toward me like someone approaching a frightened animal. "Riley, I wasn't trying to hurt you. I already told you I wasn't letting you go. Even when I go back to Oregon I will figure out a way to be with you. We can make this work."

That's just it, though; we can't make this work. I'm not supposed to have contact with people from my life before. I would be putting more people that I love in danger and I can't do that. I have to use this opportunity to push him away. I know it's a stupid reason to be mad, and I'm not really even angry at him. I'm upset about our situation. I'm angry that I can't be with the one person that I love and want to be with for the rest of my life. I got so caught up in the moment of being with him that I pushed away the real situation. I don't regret what we did and the time that we have spent together this past week, but now it's time for me to end it. Daphne's message was exactly the wakeup call I needed to bring me back to reality. I'm about to shatter both of us. Again.

I zip up my bag and stare at him. "Jayce, we can't make this work! You have to go back to Oregon, a place that I can't return to. I have to stay here! And at any time I could be moved somewhere else with a new identity. It's over, Jayce. There's no point in continuing this," I whisper as I fight the tears. I can't let him see me cry. Turning away from him, I pick up my bag and put it over my shoulder.

Jayce grabs my arm. "That's it! You're just going to give up? Don't you see it? This is our second chance! I mean, you can't tell me you don't see it. What are the chances that I end up clear across the country at the same beach as you on the same day? The chances of that happening are none, but it happened to us, Riley!" He lifts my face with his hand until our eyes lock. "I love you! Please don't run, Riley. Don't push me away."

I pull back out of his grasp. "I have to go. It's over, Jayce." I walk around him and head out the door. As I walk down the hall I hear Jayce yell, "It's not over, Riley! I'm not giving up!"

I walk faster as the tears stream down my face. My heart was just shattered to pieces, but I keep telling myself it was the right thing to do. Maybe if I tell myself it enough I'll start believing it. I walk out the front door and see Daphne sitting in the driver's seat of the car. I throw my bag into the backseat, climb into the passenger's seat and stare straight ahead. She doesn't say anything but I can feel her looking at me with concern. I'm sure I look horrible and I'm sure she knows why.

"Let's go," I say quietly.

She nods, starts the car, and backs out of the driveway. As we begin to drive away I take one last glance at the house. "Goodbye," I whisper.

***

We drive home in silence and I'm thankful Daphne doesn't try to get me to talk about it on the way home. I'm relieved when we pull into the parking lot of our apartment. I can't wait to get inside and crawl into bed and just stay there. Daphne and I climb out of the car and grab our bags. We walk into the lobby and mumble a greeting to Phil as we head for the stairs.

"Miss Riley."

I stop and turn. "Your uncle stopped by and was looking for you." I look at him confused because I don't have an uncle, which can only mean one thing. "I told him I thought you were gone but he insisted he go and see." The blood drains from my face as I realize who it was that came here. It has to be.

"D-Did he leave?" I ask once I find my voice.

"Yeah, he said he would try to catch you another time."

I turn and begin running up the stairs. Once I reach my apartment I approach it with caution. I slowly push the door open and gasp at what I see. He was here. In my apartment. There are things thrown all over and stuff moved around. He went through my belongings, probably trying to make sure he really found me.

"Riley? What's going on?" I startle as Daphne comes up next to me. I didn't even hear her come up. I look over and see her eyes widen as she takes in scene in front of her.

I sigh, "Let's get inside." I know I'm going to have to either come up with a really good lie to explain this or tell her the truth. We both slowly walk into our apartment and I turn the light on. Daphne shuts and locks the door behind us. I search the whole apartment to make sure it's empty. He definitely searched through the whole place. Every room has things thrown all over the floor and drawers and cupboards opened.

When I come back into the family room I see Daphne beginning to pick things up. I should clean the mess up but I just don't have the energy. I walk over and sit on the couch. Daphne sits next to me. I lean back on the couch and sigh. And I thought the night couldn't get any worse after we left Jayce. Daphne doesn't say anything as she waits for an explanation. I don't even know where to start.

I look over at her. "I'm sorry, Daph." And I am sorry. I'm sorry that I have now put her in the middle of my messed up situation, and maybe even danger. This was exactly why I left Jayce tonight, because I didn't want to involve anyone else.

"I don't even know where to begin." I sit up and face her. "The things I'm about to tell you and what happened tonight...you can't tell anyone." She nods and I continue, "I'm not from Iowa. We didn't move here because my dad got transferred." I take a deep breath. "I'm from Oregon."

Daphne chuckles. I look over at her with an eyebrow raised. "Sorry. I know it's not the time to be laughing and none of this is funny. I'm actually kind of freaked out about all this but I never thought you were from Iowa. Especially once we ran into Jayce." Her smile slips once she realizes whose name she just said. "Sorry, Riles, I didn't mean to..."

I hold up a hand to stop her. "It's okay."

"Daphne, I got moved here because I'm in witness protection. Almost three years ago I witnessed a murder and it involved some mob." Daphne's eyes widen as I continue. "My parents and I were put in witness protection and weren't able to contact anyone from our life before. The trial is over and all the men from the mob are behind bars, except the boss is still out there. They haven't been able to track him down and we were told that he might try to come after me since I was the reason all his men got sent to jail." By the end her eyes are as wide as saucers. We sit in silence as she looks around the room then back at me.

"And you think he was the one that came here tonight?" she asks quietly.

"Yeah."

"It all makes so much sense now. Why you don't usually get close to people. Why Jayce was so mad when he first saw you, and why you..."She doesn't finish her last statement, but I know she was going to say, *why you can't be with Jayce.* She scoots over next to me and wraps her arms around me. "I'm sorry, Riley." I begin to sob as all of the night's events catch up with me.

Frank found me, and he'll continue to come after me until he gets me. I only have one option, and it's one I didn't want to face. My only choice is telling the marshal and my parents, which means I'll probably get moved somewhere else. I'll have to leave this life just like I left the last one. It also means that I most likely won't get to see Jayce ever again. Because what are the chances of him finding me once I get moved, or us ending up at the same place at the same time again? None.

CHAPTER 17

After I calm down I look around the room and sigh. There are magazines and books tossed on the floor, the drawers in the end tables are open with papers thrown out of them. I still can't believe he found me. My phone beeps, alerting me of a text. I reach into my purse and pull my phone out, look down at the screen and gasp.

"Who is it?"

"It's from Jayce." I open the text and feel my breath catch in my throat.

Jayce: *I cannot lose, I will not fail*
For I believe love will prevail

I feel my eyes fill with tears. "I knew he wouldn't let me go," I say as I hand Daphne my phone so she can read it. She scans the message.

"What are you going to do?"

"Nothing. I can't put any more people in danger. If Ryan or Jayce ask about me I need you to just stay out of it. Jayce can't know about this. I'm going to have to tell my parents and the marshal about the break-in. I will probably be moved away again, so nobody can know about what is going on, Daph.

Please don't tell them anything that we've talked about tonight. I wasn't even supposed to tell you or Jayce, but considering our place got broken into I figured it'd be best for you to know what was going on."

"Okay, I won't."

I look around the room again and feel the tears run down my face. "I know it's late, but do you think we could stay at your brother's tonight? I don't think we should stay here, in case the guy comes back. Then tomorrow I'll go talk to my parents and probably stay there until things get figured out. You may want to stay with him for a while too."

"Yeah, I'll call him." She gets up off the couch and walks into the kitchen to call her brother. When she gets off the phone and returns she hands me a water.

"Thanks." I open it up and take a drink.

"My brother said that we could stay there tonight and I can stay as long as I need to."

I nod. "Did he ask why?" I ask quietly.

"Yeah, I told him they were going to do some work on our apartment."

"I'm sorry you had to lie to him." I look up at her. "And I'm sorry you got put in the middle of this mess now."

She walks over and sits by me. "Hey, it's not your fault. I'm here for you and will do whatever I can to help you."

"Thanks, Daph." I smile sincerely, "Well, we should probably go pack our bags." We both get up and go to our rooms. I set the bag I used to take over to Jayce's on the bed. I go over to my closet and find another bag and set it on the bed too. Then I go back to the closet and begin to pack as many clothes as I can since I don't know if I will be coming back here. I go to grab the pictures off my shelf and notice one is missing. It was a picture of me on the first day I moved into this apartment. My parents want to take pictures of me all the time since we lost everything. I search around my room for the picture, but it's nowhere to be found. The guy must've taken it, probably to make sure I'm who he is looking for.

I sigh as I pack the rest of my pictures. This night just keeps getting worse, and I have a feeling things won't get better for a while. I finish packing a few more of my things and shove them in my bags. I zip up the bags and meet Daphne in the family room.

"Got everything?" She glances down at my two suitcases.

"Oh, wait. I forgot my school stuff." I jog back to my room and grab my school bag, then return.

"Okay, now I have everything."

She nods and hoists her bags. "All right, let's go."

Daphne and I decide to drive separately so we both have a vehicle to go places. I follow her to her brother's house in Norfolk, which is only about a fifteen minute drive. I've only seen him twice. He has the same golden blond hair as Daphne, and his eyes are brown too but a darker shade. He's probably around six foot two and is very muscular. I'm not sure what he does for a living; Daphne has never told me, but whatever it is must be something that keeps him in great shape. Either that or he goes to the gym all the time.

We pull into her brother's apartment and park our cars. I get out and grab one of my bags and Daphne meets me over by my car. We walk up to the entry and Daphne knocks.

"Hey, sis!" Sean says, smiling as he opens the door.

"Hey."

Sean looks over at me and smiles. "Hey, Riley."

"Hey, thanks for letting us stay here. Sorry it's so late."

He waves his hand, "No big deal. I was up

anyway." He moves off to the side to let us pass. "Come on in."

We walk in and I glance around, noticing the layout is similar to ours. The kitchen is off to the left with the dining room just slightly to our right where he has a wooden table and four chairs to go around it. Above the kitchen sink there is an opening that looks into the family room, which is directly in front of the entryway past the dining room and kitchen.

Sean shuts the door behind us and gives us a short tour, showing us the spare bedroom down the hall where we'll be staying and the bathroom across the hall. We walk into our room and set our bags down. The room is a simple spare bedroom. It has a queen size bed with a nightstand on each side, and a small dresser against the opposite wall with a small chair next to it.

"Thanks, Sean. We are both beat. I'll see you in the morning."

"No problem. Goodnight, sis." He walks out and shuts the door behind him.

Daphne and I take turns using the bathroom to get ready for bed. Once we are both finished we turn off the light and climb into bed. We lie there in silence for a few moments.

"What happened between you and Ryan tonight?" I ask quietly.

She sighs. "Nothing. He told me that they had to leave tomorrow instead of Sunday, so I figured there was no point to stay. I mean, nothing was going to come of us anyways, so I thought why drag it out? I figured it was easier this way."

"Makes sense, I guess. Was he upset?"

"A little bit, I think. He tried to talk me into staying but didn't really fight me too much on it. It is what it is."

I nod even though she can't see me.

"I take it Jayce was mad that you left?"

"Yeah. We kind of got in a fight. I told him it was over and left."

"I'm sorry, Riley."

"It's okay," I whisper.

Neither of us say anything else and I eventually fall asleep wondering how I will survive through all of this again. Running for my life. Probably leaving this life for a new one. Leaving my friends here. And lastly, having my heart shattered to pieces again.

***

The next morning I wake up and notice Daphne isn't in the room. I get my clothes from my bag, go into the bathroom and begin getting ready for the day. I get dressed in a t-shirt and a pair of jeans, throw my hair up in a ponytail, and walk back into the bedroom. I put my things back in my bag, then grab it and go into the kitchen.

When I walk in Daphne and Sean are sitting at the table visiting and having coffee.

"Good morning. Did you sleep okay?" Daphne asks.

"Yeah, not too bad, thanks."

"There's coffee over there if you want some. The cups are in the cupboard above the coffee maker. Creamer is in the fridge," Sean says politely.

I nod, grab a cup, and pour myself some coffee. I find the creamer and pour a little in my coffee, then put it back in the fridge. I sit next to Daphne at the table; I feel awkward because I don't really know Sean that much. The times I have seen him we said like three words to each other. After a few moments of silence Sean picks up his cup and takes it over to the sink to rinse it out.

He looks over at Daphne. "I'm going to grab a shower and then I'll be ready whenever you are."

Daphne looks up from her coffee. "Okay. I'll be

ready in thirty."

Once Sean is out of the room Daphne looks over at me. "Are you going to your parents' today?"

"Yeah, I'm going after my coffee. I'll go ahead and take my stuff with me since I'll probably be staying there until I know what's going to happen. I'm going to call the marshal on the way to my parents' house too and see if he can meet us today so I can tell him what's been going on."

"Well, let me know how it goes if you can. And if there is anything I can do to help just let me know." She smiles sadly.

"I will. Thanks, Daph." I finish up my coffee, and walk over to the sink to rinse my cup out. I pick up my things and head for the door.

"I'll call you later," I say over my shoulder. "See ya."

"Bye," Daphne says as I close the door.

***

I pull up to my parents' house and my mom opens the front door and walks over to my car. She smiles and waves as she walks down the steps. I get out of the car and decide to get my bags later so I don't have to answer a bunch of questions now.

On my way here I called her to tell her I needed to talk to them about some things, and then I called the marshal and he is coming by around one o'clock. That gives me the next two hours to talk with my parents and explain everything. I'm sure they will freak out and ask why I didn't tell them any of this sooner, but honestly that would've made everything more real. I felt like if they didn't know then I could pretend I could really be with Jayce and I wasn't hiding out. I didn't have to worry about if I would be sent away again. My wakeup call was last night when I walked into my apartment and found out that

I've been found, and now my fantasy life of being with Jayce and building a relationship together is truly gone.

My mom walks over to me and gives me a hug. "Hey, honey!"

I hug her back. "Hey, Mom."

We pull back and walk up the steps to the house. "I'm surprised you stopped by today. I figured you would be spending the day at the beach with your friends. It's a nice day for it."

"Yeah, Daphne is spending the day with her brother and Gavin is out of town. Plus I needed to talk to you and Dad, so the beach can wait for another day." I put on a happy expression, trying not to worry her too much. My parents know how much I love the beach and she's right. If I didn't have such an important issue to discuss with them then the beach is exactly where I would be today.

We walk into the house to the kitchen. "Well, we're glad to have you over, honey." My mom smiles warmly at me. "I was going to fix some sandwiches for lunch. Does that sound good to you?"

I walk over and sit on the barstool at the counter. "Yeah, thanks."

My dad walks into the kitchen. "Hey, Riley." He comes over and gives me a side hug. "No beach today, huh?"

I laugh, feeling like I'm repeating myself. "No, not today. I wanted to talk to you guys about some things."

My dad sits down in the barstool next to me and my mom walks over to the counter, standing across from me. I feel my palms sweat, and start to become nervous now that my parents are both in front of me. Maybe I should just tell the marshal and leave my parents out of it. Will they be mad at me for not telling them sooner? Will they be mad because I kept in contact with Jayce while he was here? Will they be mad at me if we have to be moved again?

My dad puts his hand on my shoulder. "We're here for you, sweetheart. Whatever it is you can tell us," he says sincerely.

I nod. "Okay, but just let me get everything out before you say anything." I glance over at both of them. "Please. No interrupting."

They both nod and I begin telling them everything. I explain about when I first started feeling like I was being watched. I tell them about seeing Jayce for the first time and then running into him at the beach. I tell them about spending time with Jayce and telling him what really happened. As I go through the past week my parents' eyes continue to grow wider and they begin to look more worried. I can see they have lots of questions, but stay to their word and don't interrupt.

"Then last night Daphne and I went to hang out where Jayce and the guys are staying. Jayce and I kind of got into a fight. I told him that it wasn't going to work between us once he went back to Oregon and I ended it. I left with Daphne." I look down at the counter and begin mindlessly tracing designs on the countertop. "When Daphne and I got to our apartment Phil told us that my uncle stopped by and he insisted on going up to see if I was there." I don't look up to see my parents' expressions but I hear my mom gasp. I continue on. "I asked him if he left and he said yeah, but that the guy said he would catch me another time." I look up finally and see the worried looks on both their faces. My eyes fill with tears. "I ran up to the apartment and the guy broke in and searched through all of our things. He found me. Frank found me," I whisper and the tears begin running down my face. My parents rush over and wrap me in a hug, trying to comfort me.

After a few minutes my parents release me and go back to their previous spots, and I calm myself down enough to talk again. They spend a few minutes asking me some questions and I answer them. I tell them that I told Daphne about what was going on and that she was willing to help in any way that she could. I also tell them that I called the marshal and he would be coming over at one, so I can fill him in on everything. They were both glad about that.

Then I remember. "There's one more thing." My parents both look over at me with raised eyebrows. "I went to take all my pictures off my shelf and a picture of me is missing." I take a deep breath. "He knows it's me."

CHAPTER 18

The doorbell rings at exactly one o'clock, alerting me of the arrival of the marshal. My dad walks out of the family room to go answer the door and I lean back against the couch and close my eyes. This is it, the moment where I will get sent away again. My mom reaches over and squeezes my hand. "Everything will be okay, honey." She smiles to try to assure me but I can see the uncertainty in her eyes.

My dad walks in with the marshal following behind him.

"Good afternoon, Mrs. Anderson," he smiles as he walks over to my mom and holds out his hand.

My mom stands and shakes his hand. "Good afternoon, Mr. Miller."

He steps over to me and holds out his hand. "Miss Anderson."

I take his hand and attempt a smile. "Riley, please." I don't like being called Miss Anderson; it sounds weird to me when people call me that. Even after all this time I'm not used to our new last name. He nods and sits in the chair across from us. My dad sits on the other side of me on the couch. I watch Mr.

Miller as he pulls out a notebook and pen and begins to write some things down.

Mr. Miller is an older man, probably in his late forties. He has short brown hair with speckles of gray throughout it. He is around five-eight and a little on the heavy side. He has been our marshal since the beginning and is a pretty nice guy. We've never had any issues with him. He's always answered our questions and kept us up to date on things that we need to know.

He finishes writing then looks up. "So, Mis-I mean, Riley," he smiles, "you said you had some things to talk to me about. What's going on?"

I look over at both my parents and they both nod, letting me know to go ahead. I smile weakly at them both and turn to face Mr. Miller. I take a deep breath and tell him everything I told my parents less than two hours ago. As I'm explaining about this past week I notice him write things down every once in a while. Once I finish I watch as he scribbles more things down for several minutes. When he's done he looks up at me.

Before he can say anything I ask him the one question I've been wanting to know since last night. "Are we going to be moved again?" I ask hesitantly.

"Well, Riley, I'm not sure yet. I'm going to make a few phone calls and then I should have some answers for you." He stands and takes his phone out. "If you'll excuse me I'll go make these calls and then we can talk more about this, okay?"

We all nod and watch as he leaves the room. I look over at my parents. "Do you think we will have to move and get new identities?"

My dad wraps his arm around my shoulder. "Honestly, I don't know."

"I'm sorry that all this is happening again," I whisper and look down at the floor, feeling a little guilty for my parents having to be put in this situation again.

"Hey, don't blame yourself for this, sweetie. We don't care if we have to move again. As long as you're safe, that's all that matters. Okay?" My dad pulls me tighter against him, giving me a side hug.

My mom reaches over and holds my hand. "That's right, we just want you to be safe."

I nod and lean my head against my dad's shoulder. "Thanks, Mom and Dad."

About twenty minutes later Mr. Miller comes back into the room. I try to read his face but get nothing. It's set in a serious expression. He walks over to his chair and sits down. My parents and I sit there quietly and wait for him to speak.

"Well, I have some good news and some bad news." He glances down at his notebook then back up at us. "The good news is you won't have to relocate." We all sigh in relief.

"But the bad news is that you will all keep your current identities and live life like you have been. We haven't been able to track Frank down, so we're hoping that we can use this opportunity to finally catch him."

"What?" I gasp.

"You can't do that!" my parents say at the same time. "This is our daughter's safety you're talking about!" my father adds vehemently.

My parents begin firing off questions as I process what he just said. I'm relieved that I won't be leaving and won't have to get a new identity, but I'm terrified because that means that Frank could come after me whenever he wants. He knows where I live now, and he knows what I look like now compared to what I looked like before. I begin to feel my heart rate pick up and soon I'm breathing heavier and faster. It becomes hard to get oxygen and I feel like I'm suffocating.

My parents both look over. "She's having a panic

attack. Get her some water," I hear my mom say. She bends down in front of me. "Riley. Deep breath. Look at me, sweetie." She places her hands on my face and lifts it up to look at her. I try to inhale and focus on my mom's face.

"That's it, Riley. Another deep breath." After a few more I slowly begin to calm down. My dad comes over and hands me a glass of water. "Here, take a drink." I reach up and accept the glass from him and take a drink. I close my eyes and focus on the cold liquid going down my throat as I swallow. I take a few more swallows, then set the glass on the coffee table in front of me.

Once I calm down some I look up at Mr. Miller confused. "Why are you using me as bait? Why aren't you moving us?"

"If we moved you we would also have to move your friends that know about your circumstance as well because they could be put in danger. We don't have the funds to move everyone and give you all new identities. So we have decided that since we have been trying to find Frank for this long, the way to catch him is you. We will have a team watching you from a distance at all times to make sure you are safe. We want you to continue living your life like you normally would and pretend nothing has changed. Make sure you don't draw attention to our team that will be watching you. If Frank doesn't suspect you being watched he will probably make an attempt to come after you. Of course we will do our best to be there to catch him if he does." He looks at each of my parents and back at me. "I know this isn't what you want, but we don't have any other options. This is our chance to finally catch him. We will also have a team keep an eye on your parents and friends as well."

"Jayce is going back to Oregon and I don't want him to know anything about this. I want to keep him safe. Please don't tell him," I plead. It's better if he doesn't know. I don't want to take the chance of something happening to him.

Mr. Miller nods. "Okay, but we will still keep an eye on him too. Just in case."

"Thank you."

Mr. Miller stands and takes his notebook. "Well, I need to get going. Call me if you have any questions or any more information. I will keep you posted."

I jump up. "Mr. Miller." He glances my way. "Is it okay if I stay at my parents' house a few days or do I need to go back to my apartment?"

"You can stay here, but don't wait too long before you go back to your apartment. We don't want him to suspect anything."

"Okay, thank you." He nods and I watch as my dad walks him out.

Later that night I go up to my temporary bedroom. I close the door and lean back against it. My parents left this room pretty much how it was when I was living here. It has a double bed in the right corner of the room from the door and a five drawer dresser next to it. The walls are still the light yellow that I painted them shortly after we moved here. I thought the yellow would be cheery to wake up to every day since the rest of my life was a mess.

I close my eyes as I lean against the door. The past twenty-four hours have been crazy. I'm definitely ready for bed, although I'm not sure if I'll actually be able to sleep. After a few minutes I decide to go get ready for bed.

When I get done I retrieve my phone off the dresser and sit down on my bed. I'm sure Daphne is waiting to hear from me, so I text her.

Me: *Hey, are you able to talk?*

She calls me immediately.

"Hey, Daph."

"So what'd you find out?" she asks, getting right

to the point.

"Well, I'm not moving,"

"That's great, right?" She pauses. "Riley, why don't you sound happy about this?"

I tell her about what Mr. Miller said and why we can't be relocated again. I also explain that I am pretty much being used as bait, and they hope they will be able to catch him this way. I tell her about having a small team watching me, and also mention the men that will be watching her, Jayce, and my parents.

"Daph, please don't tell anyone about this. If Jayce tries to get in touch with you don't say a word about what's going on. He's safer if he doesn't know."

"I won't." She pauses. "This is so crazy. How are you doing with all this? Are you doing okay?" I can hear the concern in her voice.

"It doesn't really seem real, I guess. I think I'm still in shock from everything. So much has happened in last twenty-four hours that it is a lot to process."

I hear her hesitate. "Have you heard any more from Jayce?" she asks cautiously.

"No," I pause. "Have you heard from Ryan?"

"Yeah, he let me know they made it back okay." I can tell she wants to say more but she doesn't.

"Well, I'm going to try to go to bed but I will probably talk to you tomorrow."

"Okay, get some sleep. If you need anything just call me."

"Thanks. Oh, and Daph? I'll probably be going back to our place to stay tomorrow. The marshal said the sooner I get back there the better."

"All right, I'll go back tomorrow too. Goodnight."

"Night." I hit end on my phone and set it down on my nightstand. I climb under the covers and within minutes exhaustion hits me and I fall asleep.

***

I walk into my apartment after class and notice that Daphne isn't home yet. I head back toward my room to put my school books away. I open my door and freeze. This can't be happening. He can't be here. Frank is here, in my apartment, and I'm alone. My heart begins to beat faster and I begin to panic. I glance over my shoulder and begin to slowly walk out, hoping I can somehow get away and call for help.

"I wouldn't do that if I were you." His deep voice vibrates through the room.

I look back toward him and see he is pointing a gun at me. My books slam to the floor as my hands fly up to my mouth and I gasp. I'm supposed to be safe. He wasn't supposed to be able to get to me. Before I can think of what to do I hear the front door open and close.

"Riley!" Oh no. I hear footsteps getting closer and see Jayce walk into my room. Before I can react the gun goes off. I turn and see Jayce fall to the floor.

"No!" I scream. I sit up, gasping for air. I search my room frantically and realize it's still nighttime. I flip on my lamp and lean back against the headboard. It was just a dream, but it felt so real. I'm safe. Jayce is safe. Closing my eyes I focus on my breathing, trying to calm myself back down. I really hope my nightmares don't continue to come back. I'll have to make sure I get back to my kickboxing class Monday morning. That's what got me through my fears and nightmares the first time, and hopefully it will help now too.

I reach over to grab my phone off my nightstand and see it's only three o'clock. I won't be able to go back to sleep right away. I flip through my phone and pull up a picture of Jayce and me from the beach the other day. I smile sadly as I see how happy we are together. If only there was a way for us to be together. I stare at the picture, remembering all the details of Jayce's face. The way his eyes squint a little bit when he truly smiles. The slightest dimple on his right side of his face. The way his eyes light up when he is really happy, like he is in the picture. After some time I shut the screen off of my phone and sct it back on my nightstand.

I get up from the bed and quietly walk to the kitchen for a glass of water. After my trip to the refrigerator I decide to try to go back to sleep so I'm not exhausted in the morning. I climb back into bed, snuggle down into the covers, and close my eyes.

CHAPTER 19

I end up just tossing and turning the rest of the night, so trying to go back to sleep seemed pointless. Finally at six I give up and decide I need a good run. I know it's probably not the smartest thing to do after everything that has happened but I need to get out. I get up and change into a tank and some shorts, then slip on my running shoes and quietly go down the stairs.

I walk into the kitchen and startle when I see my dad by the coffeemaker. He turns around. "Oh, good morning, Riley." He looks me over. "Couldn't sleep?"

I walk over to the fridge and grab a bottle of water out of the fridge, then walk over to sit on the barstool. "No, so I'm going to go run." I open my water and take a drink.

"Do you think that is a good idea? To be out by yourself?" His brows furrow with concern.

Maybe I shouldn't have told my parents, because everything I go to do now is going to have them worried about me. I set my water down on the counter and sigh. "Dad, I know you and Mom are worried, but I'm not going to just stop going places. I can't stay cooped up inside all the time. If I do then I'm letting him control my life. I'll be fine." I get up from the stool.

He hesitates. "You're right." He comes over and gives me a hug. "It's just that we don't want anything to happen to you."

I hug him back. "I know, Dad." I pull back. "I'm going running and I'll be back in a little while. I'll have my phone with me." I smile to try to help reassure him.

"Okay, I'll see you after a bit. If you want I can fix you breakfast when you get back," he offers.

"Sounds good. Thanks, Dad." I grab my water off the counter and walk out the front door. I glance around to make sure I'm not being watched. After a few stretches I grab my earbuds and plug them into my phone. I pull up a playlist, put the earbuds in, and begin my run.

It's been a few days since I last ran, so I start off at a slower pace. I don't really know where I'm running, but I decide to stick to the residential area. I don't check to see if my "security team" is following because honestly I don't want to think about any of that. I don't want to think about the fact that Frank could decide to come after me anytime. I don't want to consider that more people I care about could be in danger. And I definitely don't want to face that the love of my life is clear across the country and I can't be with him. So instead I focus on my breathing.

Breathe in.
One.
Two.
Breathe out.
One.
Two.
Breathe in.
One.

Two.

I continue to focus on this breathing pattern as I run. After about three songs I decide to pick up my pace a little. As I run I glance around. A lot of the houses in the neighborhood are two-story family homes. The neighborhood that my parents live in has a lot of families with younger children. Most of the houses are all dark inside since it is still early and the sun hasn't began to rise yet.

I can't help but laugh at myself. Here I am running when it is dark outside and I have a murderer after me. If Frank decided to come after me right now, there wouldn't be anyone around to witness it. I must really be losing my mind, or maybe part of me doesn't want to realize the seriousness of the situation. After a while I begin to pick up my pace faster, trying to outrun all my problems. I know it sounds silly and it's impossible, but sometimes it's nice just to feel like for a moment you are truly running away from everything.

After about twenty minutes I begin heading back. The sky is beginning to lighten but it still isn't quite sunrise yet. I've always enjoyed this time of morning. I don't get up this early a lot, but when I do I try to go out and see the sunrise. It is a beautiful time of day, and it's always so quiet and peaceful.

A few blocks away from my parent's house I begin to slow for a cool down. Once I make it back the sun has begun to peek over the horizon. I stand in the driveway and do some stretches as I watch the dawn. The sky is pretty much clear with the exception of a few clouds. After my stretches I sit on the drive and look up. It's so gorgeous seeing all the shades of blues, reds, oranges, purples, and yellows.

I sit and watch the beautiful display for a few minutes, then decide to go inside. I walk into the house and go straight upstairs to the room I'm staying in. I grab jean shorts and a V-neck shirt and go into the bathroom to shower. After my shower I change into my clothes and put some mousse in my hair to leave it curly. Once I'm ready for the day I go downstairs.

As I make my way down the stairs I can smell the bacon and eggs cooking before I hear them sizzling. Walking into the kitchen I see my mom sitting on the barstool at the counter, reading the newspaper. My dad is hovering over the stove cooking the food.

"Good morning," I say as I walk over to the other barstool to sit down.

Both my parents turn toward me and smile. "Morning."

"How was your run?" my dad asks as he turns back to the stove.

"It was nice. I feel a lot better."

My mom sets down her newspaper, looks over at me. "That's good."

My dad walks over to the fridge, retrieves a water then sets it down in front of me. "Thanks," I say as I open it and take a long drink.

My dad dishes up the plates and hands them to us. We don't talk much as we eat. The food tastes so good after my run that I pretty much devour it.

When I'm done I take my plate over to the sink and rinse it off. I put it in the dishwasher and turn to face my parents. "I'm going to go back to my apartment today."

They set their forks down next to their plates and look at each other. Then they turn their concerned expressions to me. I decide to speak before they can object. "I know you are both worried about me, but like I told Dad this morning I'll be fine. I am adult and am able to make my own decisions. Mr. Miller even said to go back to the apartment sooner rather than later so it doesn't look suspicious." I walk over to the counter so I'm across from them. "Daphne is going to be coming back too so I won't be alone. I'll have her there and my 'watch' team too. See, nothing to worry about." I smile sweetly.

They both sigh before my dad speaks. "We know you're an adult, but sometimes it's hard to remember that in this situation. We just want to protect our baby."

I roll my eyes playfully. "Dad..." I sigh and he chuckles.

"Will you at least call us each day so we know that you are still safe?"

"Sure." I know this isn't easy for them either. My parents have never been ones to hover over me and be super protective, but since this whole thing began they have been. Sometimes it's annoying, but I understand it. I'm sure if I was in their situation I would be the same way.

Satisfied with my answer, they both pick up their forks and continue eating. I finish up my water and then head upstairs to my bedroom to begin gathering up my things. I'm not going to leave till this afternoon but I want to have everything together. I double check to make sure I'm not forgetting anything, then go back downstairs.

When I walk back into the kitchen I see my mom and dad cleaning up the mess.

"Hey Riley, I was thinking we could go shopping and then get some lunch afterwards while we are out. What do you think?" my mom asks as she finishes up.

"Yeah, that sounds great."

We spend the day shopping and it's a nice distraction from everything else going on. I end up with a couple new shirts, a few pairs of jeans, and a new sundress. After we finish browsing we grab some lunch at a burger place. Once we eat we go back to the house.

When we were out I did notice my "security

team" following us, so that was reassuring that I would be okay. I didn't mention anything to my mom, but I think she caught a glimpse of them too. We had a really nice time shopping and just spending some time together, just us. We haven't had a girls' day in a long time.

We pull up to the house and I look over at my mom. "Thanks, Mom. I'm glad we went shopping. It was nice to get out and get my mind off everything."

She pulls the car into the garage and puts the car in park. She looks over and smiles. "You're welcome, sweetie. I'm sure none of this is easy for you. I know it's not easy for your dad and me to watch you go through all of this." She grabs my hand and gently squeezes it. "You're a very strong and brave young woman. You have come so far since we moved here and we are very proud of you."

I feel my eyes begin to fill with tears. "Thanks, Mom. But you know I don't think I would be where I am at now if it weren't for you and Dad pushing me a little." I reach across the console and give my mom a hug. "Thank you."

She holds me tight. "You're welcome. We're always here for you if you need us." We both pull back and I wipe the tears off my cheeks.

"Let's go inside." I nod and we both get out of the car and grab our bags. I follow my mom as we walk into the house. My dad must've heard us come in because he comes into the room. "Well, did my girls have fun shopping?" He greets my mom with a kiss. He glances down at our hands full of shopping bags. "Looks like you found some things," he chuckles.

"Yeah, we had a nice time, and we both got some new outfits." My mom smiles back at my dad.

"Well, I'm going to go get my things and head back to my apartment. I have a lot to do before I go back to class and work tomorrow." I dread going back to the apartment, knowing the mess is still there from when our apartment got broken into. Daphne and I picked up a little bit the night it happened, but didn't do too much.

"Do you need any help?" my dad offers.

"No, I don't have that much. Thanks." I run out to my car and put my shopping bags in the back seat, then go back to the house to get the rest my things. Once I have everything my parents walk me out.

I give both my parents a hug. "Thanks for letting me stay."

"Anytime. You're always welcome here, you know that," my dad says and I nod.

I walk over to the driver's side and open the door. "If you need anything just call us. No matter what time, okay?" my mom says.

"I will. I'll call you guys later. Love you."

"Love you too," they reply in unison.

I get into the car and shut the door. I start the engine and begin my drive back to my apartment. On the way there I call Daphne and let her know I'm heading home. She tells me she'll meet me there so we can get our apartment put back together, something I could tell she was dreading just as much as I am. I was thankful that she was going to meet me at home because I'm actually a little nervous to go back there, and I definitely don't want to stay there by myself.

I'm so relieved that Daphne knows what is going on with my life. It's really hard to truly be friends with someone when you can't tell them things that you want to and have to lie about your past. You feel like a horrible friend because you have someone telling you things that you're assuming is true and then you tell them things about yourself that are lies. Daphne has been a great friend through all this and I'm thankful for that.

I pull into my apartment and park the car. I get

out and grab all my bags from the backseat and walk into the lobby. I say hello to Phil and he responds with a mumble and continues looking at the screens. Must be having a bad day. I walk up the stairs to my apartment and hesitate when I get to the door.

"I can do this," I mumble to myself as I put the key into the lock. I open the door and then slowly walk inside. Flipping the light on I look around the apartment. Everything looks just how we left it, or I guess how Frank left it. A disaster. Sighing, I walk into my room and begin unpacking all my bags.

I'm just hanging my new sundress when I hear Daphne come in.

"Riley! Are you here?"

I hang the dress up and walk into the family room. "Hey."

"Hey, I just have to unpack and then I'll be ready to clean."

"Sounds good. I'll go ahead and get started in here." She nods and walks off to her room.

I begin working in the kitchen, and as I'm finishing up there Daphne comes out and begins helping me. It doesn't take us long before we make our way to the family room, then back to our bedrooms. Once we are both done we collapse on the couch.

I look over at Daphne. "I don't know if I've told you this yet, but thank you." She meets my eyes and waits for me to continue. "Thank you for being understanding about this whole situation. I'm sorry that you kind of got brought into it now. If you want to move out I would understand." I don't want her to leave, but with having the apartment broken into and knowing I have someone after me, she might want to get far away from me. She needs to know that she doesn't have to stay here if she doesn't want to.

"You're not getting me out of here that easy.

Plus..." she hesitates. "That's what friends are for. Being there for each other." With the way she hesitated I think she wanted to say something different.

"Yeah, I suppose so."

"So how are your parents taking all this?"

I lean back against the couch. "They aren't happy about not being relocated. When the marshal told us that we were staying and they are using me to get Frank, my parents freaked out." I shrug. "Once he explained that I would have a security team they were a little bit better about it. Of course now they are treating me like a child. They want me checking in every day and things like that. My dad didn't think I should've gone running this morning," I sigh. "I know they are just worried, but I told them I can't live my life cooped up and not go anywhere. So hopefully they will back off a little bit."

"Yeah, I'm sure it's hard for them too. Well, hopefully this will all be over soon and they will catch the guy."

I nod. "Yeah, I hope so."

"So you want to order pizza, have some wine, and maybe watch movies?"

"Yeah, that sounds perfect, actually."

The rest of the evening we spend eating pizza, drinking wine, and watching comedies. At nine o'clock I call it a night and decide to head to bed. I didn't sleep well the night before and got up early, so I'm exhausted. After I get ready I'm just about to crawl into bed when my phone buzzes. I sit up and grab the phone off my nightstand. It's a text from Gavin.

Gavin: *Hey! I made it back from Vegas. Hope you had a good break! Want to meet up for lunch tomorrow?*

My break was great until Friday night. Of course I can't tell Gavin that, so I decide to keep it simple.

Me: *I bet you had a blast! My break was pretty good. Lunch sounds great! See you tomorrow.*

I set my alarm for six-thirty A.M so I can go to my kickboxing class in the morning, and then I set my phone on my nightstand. I roll over onto my side and   fall   asleep.

CHAPTER 20

I didn't want to get out of bed very bad this morning, but I'm definitely glad I went to kickboxing. It helped me to deal with everything from this past weekend. I showered at the gym, and made it on time for my eight-thirty class. I had two classes today and they both went fairly quickly. I got done with my last class at twelve-twenty and texted Gavin to meet me out front.

I walk out front and see Gavin sitting on the bench looking at his phone with concern. He looks up as he hears me approach.

"Hey!" Gavin smiles up at me.

"Hey. Everything okay?"

"Oh. Um...yeah," he says quickly. He stands and places his phone in his pocket. "You ready?"

"Yep. I have until two-thirty." We begin walking toward the parking lot.

"Sounds good. So where do you want to eat?"

"How about that sub place down the street?"

"Sure. I'll drive." I almost agree but then remember I have people following me. I don't know if it's a problem to ride in someone else's car. I wouldn't think so but decide to play it safe.

I grab Gavin's arm as he heads toward his truck. "Actually, I'll drive this time." He stops and looks back. "If that's okay," I smile.

He hesitates a second but then nods. "Okay." I know he prefers to drive but the way he hesitated, it seems odd.

We turn to head toward my car. "So how was Vegas?" I ask.

"It was good. We stayed right on the strip so that was cool."

"Who'd you go with again?"

We walk up to my car and I unlock the doors. "Matt and a few other guys," he says as he climbs into the passenger seat. I open the door and get into the driver's seat. "So did Daphne drag you out to the clubs all week?" he asks, changing the subject quickly.

I begin driving toward the sub place. I don't know if I should tell him all the details about running into my ex and hanging out with him all week or just keep things simple. It sounds so weird calling Jayce my ex since we never officially broke up. I decide to keep things simple since I have enough complications going on in my life right now. No need to bring other people into it. "We went to the club a few times and spent a lot of time at the beach here since it was warmer."

"No crazy stories to tell me?" he chuckles.

Ha, if he only knew how crazy things were. Of course I'm not going to tell him. "Nope, we were good little girls." I smile innocently and bat my eyelashes at him for added effect.

He laughs, relaxing a little more. "I don't know about that."

I smack him on the shoulder. "Whatever! Daphne and I don't do crazy things."

That just makes him laugh harder. "What about

on your twenty-first birthday?"

I blush, remembering what he is talking about. Of course I didn't know what was going on at the time since I was too drunk.

"I mean, who forgets their address?" He shakes his head, still laughing.

Definitely not a moment I'm proud of or like to be reminded of. I don't think he will ever let me forget that night. I was so drunk that I couldn't remember my address and I ended up giving the cab driver the wrong one. Daphne was with me but she had passed out. The driver took us to the location I gave him, and I don't even know where I came up with it. Once I got both of us out I realized it wasn't my apartment, so I called Gavin and had to ask him for my address. So embarrassing. He thankfully knew what my address was. I ended up stopping the cab before it left and was able to get a ride back to my apartment.

We pull into the restaurant and I put the car in park. I look over at Gavin and narrow my eyes. "One of these days I will have a blackmail story for you. Just wait and see."

"Yeah, we'll see, Riles." He chuckles, "We'll see." He opens his door and gets out of the car. I do the same and we walk into the restaurant together.

We both order our subs and have a nice lunch together. We catch up on what's happened over the last week, excluding Jayce and Ryan. He tells me a few stories about his trip but seems to be holding some things back. During our lunch he checks his phone several times and looks around outside, almost like he's looking for someone. I ask him again if everything is okay, and he assures me that everything's fine. I decide to let it go for now and just enjoy our lunch together.

We finish eating and walk out to my car. "So you have to work today?" Gavin asks as he opens his door and gets in the car. I do the same. "Yeah, at

three until six, so it's a pretty short shift today."
Almost too short to go in, but hey, every little bit
helps I suppose.

"That's cool. Do you and Daphne have plans this
weekend?"

I start the car and begin the short drive back to
campus. "I don't think so."

"Matt and the guys are talking about going out
this weekend if you and Daphne want to come."
Going out now doesn't sound as appealing now that
my life is in danger; anyway I was never really big on
partying in the first place.

"I don't know. I'll talk to Daphne and see if she
wants to go." Hopefully she doesn't, but she's always
up for going out, so we'll see I guess. Of course, after
everything that's happened she might not want to.

I pull up to Gavin's truck to drop him off. "All
right, well, just let me know. I'll talk to you later." He
opens the door and climbs out.

"Hey, Gavin?" He leans back into the car.
"Thanks for lunch."

"No problem. Have fun at work." He shuts the
door, waves, then walks over to his truck. I pull away
and begin driving to work.

I think back to my lunch with Gavin and can't
help but wonder what is bothering him. He seemed
different. His smiles seemed a little forced and never
quite reached his eyes. If I didn't know him as well as
I do then I probably wouldn't have picked up on it.
I'd thought about asking him if he was waiting for
someone to call or show up but decided not to.

I'm glad to be back to my normal schedule of
work and class. It's only the first day back, but it
keeps me busy and not worrying about the fact that
I'm in danger. Going back to a routine helps me to
feel like my life is somewhat normal instead of a
disaster. In some ways I feel like last week being able
to see and spend time with Jayce all seems like a

dream. If it was a dream then the end definitely turned into a nightmare.

I pull into work and park the car. I turn the ignition off, lean back against my seat, and sigh. This is a good thing. Going back to my regular routine of going to class and to work. I need this. It helped me get through all this the last time, so surely it will help me this time too. I grab my purse and head into work.

When I walk in I see Sally at the front desk. She hears me approach, looks up and smiles. "Hey, Riley! How was your weekend?"

"Hey, Sally. It was good, but it's nice to be back to work again." I smile and walk to the backroom to put my things away. When I return to the desk Sally hands me some files and I get right to work. The three hours goes by quickly, and before I know it it's time to go home.

As I walk to my car my phone begins to ring. I look down and see it's Daphne.

"Hey!"

"Hey! Are you going to be home for dinner? I'm making spaghetti and needed to know how much to fix."

"Yeah, I just got to my car." I unlock the door and get in.

"Great! See you when you get here. Bye." She hangs up before I can even say goodbye. Weird. I glance down at my phone and see that I have several missed calls. I open it up and almost drop my phone. They are all from Jayce. I haven't heard anything from him since Friday night. I see that I have two voicemails from him too. I decide to wait to listen to them because I know that once I hear his voice I will break down crying. I'm not ready to hear what he has to say yet.

On my drive home I begin wondering what Jayce had to say. I know he said he wasn't giving up, but I haven't heard from him. I'd hoped that once he got back to Oregon he would just go back to how things were before he came here. After the way I left things though, I knew he meant what he said. I'm a block away from my apartment when my phone begins to ring again. I glance at the screen and see Jayce is calling again. My eyes flick back and forth between the road and my phone, debating on if I should answer it.

After a couple rings I silence the phone and set it back on the seat. A minute later it beeps, letting me know Jayce left another voicemail. It's better this way. He's safer this way. He doesn't need to be dragged into this mess any further. We had a nice week together, but now we need to go back to living our lives how it was before. Maybe if I keep telling myself this over and over again I will eventually believe it. Highly doubtful, but worth a shot, right?

I pull into my apartment, thankful to finally be home. I get my things and walk up to my apartment. When I open the door I'm greeted with the smell of oregano and garlic. I feel my stomach instantly growl in response.

"Hey," I say to Daphne as I walk by the kitchen. "Smells good."

"Thanks." She continues facing the stove, stirring the sauce and busying herself with dinner.

I walk back into my room and put my things away. When I walk back to the kitchen Daphne is grabbing the plates out of the cupboard. I take a plate from her. "Thanks for making dinner," I remark as I dish up my food. "Hey, have you talked to Gavin since he's been back?"

"No problem. No, I haven't. Why?" She gets her food after me and we both walk over to the table.

"Just seemed like something was bothering him, I guess. I didn't know if he said anything to you." I set my plate down and retrieve two waters from the fridge. "Want one?"

"Yeah, thanks. No, he hasn't said anything." I set the bottles on the table and sit down across from her. We both begin to eat in silence. I glance up at Daphne after several minutes and notice how focused she is on her food. I sit there and watch her a minute and she continues eating without looking up. She is hiding something. I can tell. She acted weird on the phone, made one of my favorite meals, and since I got home she hasn't made eye contact.

I set my fork down. "Daphne."

She startles, almost like she forgot I was here, and looks up at me.

"Is everything okay?" I ask with raised eyebrows.

"Yeah. Everything's fine. Why?" She still doesn't quite meet my eyes.

"You're lying. You can't even look me in the eyes." I laugh a little.

She sighs and sets her fork down. "Okay, but please don't freak out on me, okay?"

I narrow my eyes. "Okay…"

"Jayce called me." I begin to say something, but she holds her hand up for me to stop and continues. "He got my number from Ryan. He said he tried calling you but you wouldn't answer. He knows he's being watched and didn't know why. Then he became worried about you and if you were okay. When you didn't answer he called me." She looks at me nervously.

"What did you tell him?" I ask slowly.

"Well, of course he didn't come right out and tell me he was being watched. He asked me different questions, trying to ask me without giving away anything about you. I finally just told him that I knew because I wanted him to get to the point. So then he told me and asked if I knew why he was being followed and if you were still being watched." She looks away and hesitates.

"You told him what happened, didn't you?" I snap a little too harshly. I'm not trying to get mad, but I told her not to tell him. I need him to be safe, which means away from me. If Jayce knows I'm in danger he may decide to come back here and I can't let him do that.

She looks back at me, her face angry. "What was I supposed to say, Riley? He was worried about you!" she snaps. "I kept telling him that you were fine but he didn't believe me. He knew that something was going on and he wouldn't drop it. So I finally just told him."

I lean back in my chair. Of course he wouldn't let it go. That's how Jayce is. He gets what he wants and won't stop until he does. I look over at Daphne, feeling bad about overreacting. "I'm sorry I snapped at you. It's just I didn't want him to know because I knew he would be worried. I want him to stay there so I know he is safe."

"I know. I'm sorry I told him but I tried not to. I really did."

"He is pretty persistent." I smile a little, thinking about how tenacious he can be. "So what did he say?"

"He was pretty upset about it. He talked about taking the first flight out here but I told him that was a bad idea. I talked him out of it which took a while. I told him that you had a team watching you too, and I would be with you most of the time. I also told him that you would want him to finish off the semester and would be mad if he came back here and missed school."

"So I'm assuming that's why he's been calling me all afternoon."

"Probably." She hesitates a moment. "So are you going to call him back?"

"I don't know. I think it's safer if I don't have any contact with him, just in case. I mean, Frank found out I was here somehow, so who knows what other information he could get?"

"Yeah, I guess that makes sense," she agrees sadly.

I pick my plate up from the table, having lost my appetite, and go rinse it off. I help clean up the dinner mess and put the leftovers in the fridge. After we're all done I tell Daphne, "I'm going to go try to do some reading and then go to bed. I'll see you in the morning."

"All right, see you in the morning, Riles," she replies apologetically.

When I get to my room I go to my bed and collapse. I see my phone flashing, so I pick it up and turn the screen on. I have another missed call from Jayce but he didn't leave a voicemail this time. I decide I should probably at least listen to his voicemails.

I play the first one.

"Riley, it's Jayce. I just wanted to make sure you were okay. Call me when you get this. I need to talk to you."

Now the second one.

"Riley! I just talked to Daphne. Why didn't you tell me what happened?" He sounds angry, which I can understand. He's silent a moment, then he sighs into the phone. *"I'm sorry, Riley. I should be there with you. I shouldn't have let you go that night. I should've gone after you. Please call me."*

Next the third.

"Riley, I know you're ignoring my calls now. I just want to hear for myself that you're okay. I love you. Ignoring me isn't going to change that. I meant what I said Friday night. All of it. Please call me back."

I don't realize I'm crying until a tear falls onto the screen of my phone. I miss him so much. I know I probably should call him, but I know once I talk to him I will beg him to come back. I set my phone on my nightstand and continue telling myself he is safer in Oregon.

I get ready for bed quickly and crawl between the sheets. Once I'm settled I listen to his voicemails over and over again as I lay there and sob. I don't know how long I cry for, but I eventually fall asleep holding my phone in my hand.

CHAPTER 21

I ended up being ten minutes late for class the next morning but thankfully no one really noticed today. My professor just continued lecturing as I slid into a seat in the back of the room. I grab out my notebook and pen, then open my textbook to the page we are on. I find a clean sheet of paper and begin taking notes as my professor talks the rest of class.

My eyes were all red and swollen this morning from crying again all night. Thanks to some makeup I don't look as bad. I've done so much crying this past week that I'm surprised I have any tears left to cry. I still haven't decided if I should call Jayce back or not. I'm not trying to purposely hurt him by ignoring him, but I'm trying to keep him out of danger. And if keeping him safe means not communicating with him then that's what I will do. I'm considering calling Mr. Miller to see what he thinks I should do, because right now I don't feel like I'm in a good position to make an objective decision.

I'm startled out of my thinking when I notice people around me packing up their things and walking out the door. I look down at my notebook and realize I stopped taking notes partway through class. Lovely. I close my textbook and pack up my things. I follow the crowd into the hall and head to my next class. Hopefully I'll be able to pay better attention in this one. I'm just about to walk into the room when I feel someone lightly grab my arm. I scream.

"Whoa! Riley, it's me." Gavin turns me around and looks me over. His face turns to concern. "Are you okay?" He pulls me out of the way so other students can get in the door. I look around and realize several people are giving me weird looks. Great, just what I need...more attention drawn to myself.

I sigh. "Yeah, I'm fine. You just startled me, that's all." I force a smile, trying to convince him.

Of course he doesn't buy it. "That's not all. You walked right by me and I tried calling your name to get your attention, but you still kept on walking." I guess I'm more out of it than I thought.

"I just have a lot on my mind right now but I'll be fine." I nod my head toward the classroom. "But I need to get in there. I'll text you later."

I can see him hesitating whether or not he should let this go. "Gavin, really, I'm fine."

"Okay." He starts walking backward, still watching me. "Text me later." I nod and turn around to walk into class.

My next lecture isn't much better than the first. I ended up spacing out through that one too. I got some of the notes down but missed pretty much the second half of the lecture. When I walk out of my second class Daphne is waiting outside the door for me.

"Let me guess. Gavin texted you?"

"Yep. He said he was worried about you."

I begin walking toward the parking lot and Daphne falls into step with me.

"Isn't everyone?" I mumble. I'm worried about myself too. I don't even feel like myself. I feel like I'm negative about everything and I cry so much now. My emotions are all over the place. I don't want to go back to how I was when we first moved here, but I'm beginning to feel like that's what's happening.

"Hello? Riley? Did you hear what I said to you?" Daphne waves her hand in front of my face.

I stop and face her. "No, I'm sorry. What did you say?"

"I said maybe you should take the rest of the day off."

"I can't. I'm supposed to be at work in thirty minutes."

"I know. I think you should call in. No offense, but you don't look so good. Did you eat anything?"

"No, but I'm not really that hungry."

She grabs my hand and pulls me. "Let's go. I'll drive you home and we'll get you some food. You need to eat." I follow behind her, knowing she won't let me win on this. Probably wouldn't be a good idea to go in to work if I've been spacing out all day anyway.

When we get into her car I pull out my phone and call the clinic to let them know I won't be able to make it in. They said not to worry about it because they didn't have a lot for me to do anyway. Once I'm off the phone I look over and see Daphne watching me closely.

"Riley. Are you sure you're okay? You can talk to me, you know?"

"Honestly, I don't know. I think everything has finally hit me," I say quietly. I turn and stare out the window. It's a bright and sunny day outside, so cheerful looking. I watch as people walk to and from their cars, laughing and talking with their friends like they don't have a care in the world. Completely the opposite of how I feel. "I spaced out in both of my classes. I only got part of the notes down. I walked right by Gavin in the hall and he called out to me and I didn't even notice him. I screamed when he grabbed my arm." I turn to face her. "I'm scared, Daph. He's out there somewhere and knows where I am."

"Is there someone you can talk to? You know, to help you work through all this?"

"Yeah, I saw a counselor a little while after we first moved here."

"Did it help?" she asks quietly.

"Yeah, I think so."

"Maybe you should go talk to your counselor then. I mean, you've been through a lot and I think anyone in your position would break down. I'm still a little freaked out by the whole thing and I didn't even go through it."

"Yeah, I think I will. I only have seven weeks left of school before I graduate and I can't afford to mess up now. I need to be focused." I decide I'll call my counselor tomorrow to set up an appointment.

"Good, now let's go get you some food. Then we'll be lazy the rest the night." She grins, then starts the car.

As Daphne turns out of the parking lot I rest my head on the window, wondering if this mess will ever be over. After a couple minutes something catches my eye. I look in the side mirror and notice a black SUV with tinted windows coming up on us fast. Realizing they aren't slowing down I feel myself start to panic.

"Daph! I think we're being followed." I panic.

She glances up in the rearview mirror and her eyes widen. "I think you're right. Hold on!"

Before she can get away I'm jerked forward and smack my head on the dash.

"Riley?"

Dazed, I slowly look over at Daphne but she is

focused on the road in front of her.

"Riley? Are you okay?" Concern is laced with a little bit of panic in her voice.

I reach up to touch my head and wince. "I-I'll be fine. What happened?"

She takes a quick glance at me and then turns back to the road, "We got rear-ended by that black SUV." I look around and realize that we are moving at a very high speed. Daphne is weaving us in and out of traffic, almost like she's done this more than once. Has Daphne gone through something like this before? Was Daphne ever in danger? Shouldn't she be freaking out right now? This isn't the Daphne I am familiar with. This is a side of Daphne I'm not sure I've ever seen. Looks like Daphne has her own secrets. I look over and study her a moment. At first glance she seems calm, then I see the tight, white-knuckled grip on the steering wheel and realize maybe she is just as freaked out as I am.

She glances in the rearview mirror quickly, "I think we lost them." I turn around and don't see anyone following us, then glance around and notice that we aren't heading toward our apartment.

"Where are we going? We should probably stay somewhere else tonight until I talk to Mr. Miller."

Daphne nods. "Yeah, I was thinking a hotel."

As we drive to the hotel in silence I can't help but think that Frank was behind this. It had to be him; he wants me gone. He must've been watching me on campus and seen me get in Daphne's car. Then another thought hits me. Where was my security team through all this? Their job is to keep me safe. I decide the first thing I need to do when we get to the hotel is call Mr. Miller.

When we get to the hotel Daphne orders us room service while I make the phone call to my marshal. After the call I go sit on the bed next to Daphne who is laying down. She hands me a bag of ice and I place it gently on my forehead. We sit, not speaking for several minutes before I break the silence. "I talked to the marshal. I think Frank was involved somehow—it's the only thing that makes sense. The marshal is looking into it some more, but he doesn't think they'll be able to trace it back to him." I pause, thinking back on what Mr. Miller said. "The security team saw the SUV rear-end us but then somehow lost both vehicles in the chase. They were able to get the license plates though. They came back registered to someone else—turns out the vehicle was stolen." I sigh. "A security team will be staying here at the hotel keeping watch, and then they are also going to continue to keep an eye on our apartment tonight too. Tomorrow we should be able to stay at our place again." Not that I'll feel any safer there after what happened last week and then today. "I'm sorry, Daph. I'm sorry about your car, and everything else that involves this mess." Knowing that Daphne's life was put in danger today because of me causes my eyes to fill with unshed tears. I shake my head trying to hold them back, not wanting to cry over this anymore.

She props herself up on her elbows and locks eyes with me. "Don't be sorry about any of this, Riley. None of this is your fault. I don't care about my car. The important thing is we're both okay and safe now."

I study her a moment. "Are you okay? Did you get hurt?"

"My neck is a little sore, but nothing major. I took a couple ibuprofen. I'll feel fine soon." Daphne gets up and walks over to the small table. "We should probably eat."

I look over and notice the food on the table; it must've arrived when I was on the phone. We both get our food and sit. As I'm eating I remember how calm Daphne was and how well she handled the car chase.

"Daphne?" I wait until she looks up, "You don't have to tell me, but how are you so calm through all this? Even when we were being chased you seemed like you knew what you were doing. Then when our apartment got broken into...I don't know. I guess I figured you would freak out or something."

"Someday I'll explain it to you, but for now I'll keep it simple." She pauses and I notice her eyes begin to glisten. "Let's just say I know what it's like to have my life in danger," she says quietly as she looks down at her food.

I'm stunned. I never would have guessed. I don't know what to say so I nod and we go back to eating in silence. I've known Daphne for a couple years now; she has always seemed to be so put together and happy. If she knows what it is like to be in danger then I'm sure being involved in my situation brings back memories of before for her, and it makes me feel guilty. I want to apologize to her, but I know she wouldn't let me feel responsible for all this.

We spend the rest the evening watching TV and making light conversation. It isn't until we are both lying in bed that I remember that Jayce had been trying to call me yesterday. I'm sure he's worried since he hasn't heard back from me.

"Hey, Daph...um, did you end up talking to Jayce again?"

"Yeah, he called me this morning. I figured you hadn't called him back since he was calling me so I answered. I told him again that you were fine and that you're worried that the guy could get access to your phone records, and that's why you probably aren't calling him back."

"Thanks. I want to talk to him...I really do. I just feel like everything I do right now could be watched or monitored, and then I'd put others in danger too. I wouldn't be able to handle it if someone I loved and cared about got hurt because of me." I feel my eyes begin to water and I reach up and wipe them. "Right now I just feel like it's safer this way," I whisper, trying to fight the tears.

"Do you want me to tell him that?"

"Yeah, if you wouldn't mind." I don't want Jayce to think I don't want to talk to him. I know that we texted while he was here but that was before I knew for sure that Frank was watching me and that he found me. Now I need to take all the precautions I can, which reminds me. "And please don't say anything about what happened today. I can't have him coming out here. If he was freaked out about the break-in, I can't imagine what he would do if he found out about today."

"Okay, I won't."

"Thanks."

***

The next month and a half goes by quickly. I've been going to see my counselor regularly. The first month I was going twice a week but now I only go once a week. I am doing a lot better and staying busy. I have been focusing only on school and work. Daphne and Gavin both have asked me to go out, but I just haven't wanted to go out to the clubs. I think Daphne just wanted me to go to try to take a night off from everything going on in my life, but I still feel it's too risky. I do spend my weekends at the beach mostly since it has been warmer, so it's not like I don't go do anything.

I haven't heard anything more from Jayce, but Daphne did tell me that she talked to him and explained why I didn't answer his calls. She said he wasn't happy about it, but for now he wouldn't call me. When we talked about it, it seemed like she wasn't telling me everything, but I just let it go.

Mr. Miller tried to look into the black SUV but he came up with nothing. They did find the black SUV later, but no sign of Frank. After the car chase Mr. Miller put more people on my security team in hopes that we wouldn't have any more problems. I haven't had any more creepy feelings of being watched, our apartment hasn't been touched, and I haven't had any more car chases, but I know this isn't over.

There have been a few times that I have gotten a phone call from an unknown number. When I answer it the line is silent. Last week I had a note on my windshield that said *You won't always have your guards around...this isn't over.* I have been trying to stay strong through all of this, but seeing those words terrifies me. I know that Frank wouldn't go through all this trouble of finding me and then not try to follow through with anything, but seeing him confirm it through a threat makes it more real. I've talked to Mr. Miller a few times. I've told him about the phone calls and the note, but none of it traced back to Frank and they still haven't been able to find him either. Apparently Frank knows what he's doing, which makes him more dangerous. Now we are all on edge, waiting for him to show up.

Today is my last day of finals and then I graduate on Saturday. I'm so excited to finally be done. I've been working hard this last month and a half to keep my grades up. As long as I do well on my finals I should end up with three A's and one B for the semester. All my hard work is paying off.

I took off work this whole week so that I could study for my finals. Also I wanted a short break before I get started full time. Starting next week I'll be working full time instead of part time. They still don't have any openings for an assistant yet, but my boss told me that soon they might need to hire another one since we are getting more patients. I enjoy the people that I work with so for now I will continue working there as the receptionist.

I walk into the kitchen and pour myself a cup of coffee.

"Hey, can you pour me a cup too?" Daphne comes in and I grab another cup and pour her some. "So are you excited to be done after today?"

I pick up our cups and walk over to the table. I place Daphne's cup down in front of her and then sit down across from her and grin. "Yeah, I almost just want to skip my last two finals," I laugh.

"I'm a little jealous. I still have another year to go."

"Yeah, I'm sure it will go by fast though."

"I hope so," she sighs.

"So do you want to go out to eat somewhere and celebrate tonight?" she offers.

"Yeah, that sounds great."

"Good, because I already told Gavin and Matt that we were going so you can't change your mind now."

I laugh, "Of course you did." I finish up my coffee and walk over to the sink to rinse the cup out. "I know I asked you awhile back but do you think Gavin is acting weird?"

"What do you mean by weird?"

"I don't know. He's been acting different. It's like something is really bothering him. I've tried to ask him about it but he avoids the question."

She shrugs. "Maybe he's just been stressed with finals and finishing up this semester."

"Yeah. Maybe." Although I don't think that is really what it is. It seems like a bigger deal than that. He's been like this since he got back from his Spring Break trip. He checks his phone all the time. He hasn't been as laidback and seems tense. When we go places or on campus he is always looking around, almost like he is looking for someone. I don't mention any of this to Daphne since she hasn't seemed to notice these changes. Maybe I'm just overthinking it.

"Well, I need to get going but I will see you tonight."

"Yep. I won't get out of my last class until three but then I should be home."

I get my things off the couch and walk over to the door. "All right. See you then." I head down to my car.

As I'm walking across the parking lot to my car I feel a familiar chill run down my spine. It's been almost two months since I've felt this but it's a feeling I wouldn't forget. I know I'm being watched by my security team but this feeling is different. I don't know how I can tell the difference but I just can. I stop at my car and look around casually. Off a little ways to my right I see one of the guys from the security team watching me. I look around in the other directions and don't see anything else out of the ordinary. I glance around one more time, thinking maybe I missed something but still nothing.

Deciding that maybe I am just being paranoid I unlock my car and get in. I start my car and look down at the clock on the dashboard. I don't have time to dwell on it now; I'm already running a little late. I put my car in drive and head toward campus.

After doing a little speeding I ended up making it to class right on time. My last two finals go quickly and before I know it I'm officially done. At twelve-fifteen I walk out of my last class and see Gavin walk out of his class across the hall. I begin walking toward him but all of sudden my vision gets blurry and I feel light-headed. I begin to feel myself stumble and am caught by two strong arms. Gavin catches me and places me back on my feet. He pulls me off to the side. "Hey, you okay?" He begins to look me over, his brows furrowed in concern.

"Yeah, I just got a little lightheaded, that's all."

"You look really pale. Here, let's go get you some

water and sit down." He grabs my hand and pulls me toward the student center. As we're walking I begin to feel nauseous. I glance up ahead and see we're close to the bathroom.

"Gavin, I think I'm going to be sick." He looks at me a little panicked, then sees the bathroom up ahead.

"Okay, let's get you to the bathroom." We pick up the pace and my stomach begins to feel queasier. Once we get to the bathroom I sprint into a stall. I just barely make it to the toilet when I begin throwing up. Once the nausea passes I flush the toilet and walk out of the stall. I grab a paper towel, get it damp and wipe off my face.

I stare in the mirror, and understand why Gavin was concerned. I look really pale. I turn on the cold water and splash some on my face, hoping it will help somehow. I dry my face off and walk out of the bathroom. When I get out of the bathroom I see Gavin leaning against the wall holding a water. When he hears me approach he looks up with relief. "Feel any better?" He hands me the bottle.

"A little. I still feel lightheaded. Thanks for the water."

"You still look pretty green. Let's stop by the walk-in clinic down the street. I'll drive you." He begins walking but I grab his hand, "Gavin, I'll be fine. It's probably the flu or something."

"Well, we can know for sure once we go to the clinic. Let's go. I'm not taking no for an answer."

"So bossy," I mumble and he chuckles as I follow him out to his truck.

CHAPTER 22

When we get to the clinic I only have to wait fifteen minutes before they call me back. I'm actually kind of glad that Gavin brought me here. There have been a few times I've felt lightheaded and nauseous the past week, but never actually threw up. I didn't tell Gavin that because he was concerned enough. I'm sure it's nothing major, probably the flu or something.

I'm sitting in the examination room waiting for the doctor to come in. The nurse took all my vitals and got a urine sample, so now I'm waiting to see if they figured out what's wrong. The nurse said that my blood pressure was a little low, which would have caused me to feel lightheaded.

There's a knock on the door before the door opens.

"Good afternoon, Riley. I'm Dr. Williams." He looks down at my chart. "So you've been feeling lightheaded and nauseous."

"Yeah, I threw up too."

"Is today the first time you've had these symptoms?"

"Well, it's the first time I've actually thrown up, but I've felt like this a few times this last week. I figured it was from not eating as much. I haven't had much of an appetite." I haven't wanted to eat for the past month and a half and have actually lost a little bit of weight. I figured it was from all the stress of everything going on so I haven't been too concerned.

He nods and looks up at me. "Riley, when was your last period?"

I find that question a little odd and personal, but I try to think of when I last had my period. I've had so much going on that I can't remember when I had it last. I look over at him. "I don't remember. Why?"

He sets my chart down on the counter and sits down across from me. He gives me a long look. "Riley, the reason you're having these symptoms is because you're pregnant."

Clearly I must've heard him wrong, "Tha-that's not possible. I haven't...." The memory of my last night with Jayce comes to mind. Oh no. How is that possible? We were safe. He didn't have any protection but I was on the pill. Isn't the pill supposed to be like ninety-nine percent effective or something?

"Are you sure? There was only one time recently and that was a month and a half ago, and I'm on the pill. It's supposed to be effective and prevent this. Right?"

"Yes, I'm sure. The pill is a form of birth control, but there is still a small chance that you still can get pregnant."

"This can't be happening," I whisper. It's not that I don't want kids. I do. Back in Oregon I always imagined Jayce and I could someday get married and have a family. But now Jayce is clear across the country. My life is in danger and I didn't want to bring Jayce into that. I've been trying to keep him safe. Now I have a baby to think about. Our baby. What am I going to do?

"If you want we can talk about what options..."

"No! I'm keeping it! I'll figure it out." I get up and grab my things. "Can I go now?" I don't mean to be rude and snap at him but I need to leave. I don't want to be here anymore. I need to get home.

"Yes, I recommend you set up an appointment with an obstetrician as soon as you can. They'll be able to help you figure out how far along you are and answer any questions that you may have."

"Okay, thank you." I walk out the door and head for the lobby. When I get there I walk over to the counter and make sure I don't need to sign out or anything. I turn around to leave and run into Gavin.

"Hey, how'd it go?" I completely forgot Gavin was here. I can't tell him. I'm not ready to tell anyone.

I look up at him and give a weak smile. "Yeah, I was just dehydrated. I need to drink more fluids and I'll be fine."

"Good. I'm glad it's nothing major." His phone buzzes, alerting him of a text. He pulls it out to read it and tenses. He glances up at me before typing out a response then he shoves his phone back in his pocket. "Ready to go? I'll take you home."

"Yeah, but can you drop me off at my car instead?"

He hesitates and looks me over. "Yeah, I can do that."

We both walk out to his truck and get in. He drives me over to my car. I open the door and get out, then turn toward him. "Thanks for helping me out and taking me to the clinic."

"No problem. I'm glad you're feeling better."

"Thanks! See you tonight." I begin to shut the door, "Riley!"

When I turn to meet his gaze he seems unsure. He looks almost worried. I'm about to question him when he stammers "I'm...I just..." He shakes his head. "Never mind. I'll see you tonight!" His smile doesn't quite reach his eyes. I smile and nod, then shut the door.

Getting in my car, I wonder what Gavin was going to say to me. It seemed like he was having an internal battle about if he should tell me or not. I try to think of what could have Gavin so worried, but come up empty. I know he's been different since he got back from his trip. For now I decide to just wait it out. At the moment I have more pressing things to worry about.

On the drive home I finally let the reality of my situation sink in. I'm going to be a mom. That both excites me and terrifies me. I'm excited because it gives me a little hope that maybe Jayce and I can start a life together like I always wanted. But what if Jayce isn't ready to settle down and start a family? Is he going to be upset with me? Will he be happy?

Then there is the main concern. Frank. I'm terrified because Frank is still out there trying to kill me. I don't know how I'm going to be able to keep me and a baby safe. Hopefully all this will be over before the baby comes; if not then I'll figure it out when it gets closer. For now I need to figure out when and how I'm going to tell Jayce.

I get back to my apartment and as I'm walking in the lobby I feel my phone vibrate in my pocket, alerting me of a text. I pull my phone out and read the text.

Daphne: *Hey! I'll be done with class earlier. I should be home in the next 30 min. Want to go to the beach for a bit?*

Once I'm up the stairs I type out a response.

Me: *Sounds great! See you soon.*

I smile as I put my phone back in my pocket. I think going to the beach is the perfect option. It always helps to clear my mind, and right now I need that. I may even tell Daphne what I found out. She might be able to help me figure out what I should do.

I grab my keys out of my purse. I put the key in but when I go to turn it I notice the door is already unlocked. Weird. Daphne must've forgot to lock the door. I go into the apartment and walk over to fridge to get a water. I'm starting to feel a little better since I drank the one that Gavin gave me, and figure once I have another I'll be better. I take a long drink before I start to walk into the family room.

When I get to the family room I freeze and the water slips through my hand and spills on the floor. I blink a couple times to make sure I'm seeing clearly. When the scene doesn't change I feel the blood drain from my face. I'm supposed to be protected. I'm supposed to have people watching me so this doesn't happen. I feel myself begin panicking. My breathing begins to pick up and my heart beats faster. This can't be happening.

There sitting on my couch is my worst nightmare. I've never actually seen him in person but I was showed pictures of him. He looks pretty much the same as he did in those photos. Today he's dressed in a black suit as if he was going to a business meeting. He has slicked back dark brown hair, almost black with streaks of gray throughout. He's probably in his fifties or so. I can see his face has aged a little in the past couple years. I look up into his gray eyes and he smirks. "Hello, Riley. Or should I call you Elizabeth?" His deep voice sends chills down my spine. "Nice hair, by the way. I almost didn't recognize you."

"H-how did you get in here?" I ask and I can hear the fear in my own voice. By the smile on his face he heard it too.

He grins. "Well, it was easy, really. Your security team isn't very useful when they are playing with their cell phones all the time. It was easy for me to slip on by and then wait for the guy down in the lobby to get busy doing something else." I knew the security team had been slacking off a bit since it had been a month and a half with nothing but dead ends. They probably assumed nothing was really going to happen but I knew better.

"Why go through all this trouble to come after me? I didn't do anything."

His grin falls and his face turns serious. I can see the hatred, coldness, and anger in his eyes. "See, that's where you're wrong. It's because of you," he points his finger at me and glares, "that all my men are behind bars. If it weren't for your testimony I would still be in business." I feel myself beginning to shake. This can't be it for me. I have a baby to think about now. I need to find a way out of this. As he's talking I remember that my phone is still in my pocket. If I can distract him while I call Mr. Miller on speed dial, he might be able to get his men up here before it's too late.

I slowly back up to the wall and lean against it. I feel like it's that night at the gas station all over again. I move my hands behind me and slowly reach for my phone. "Why don't you just start your business over again?" I ask innocently.

His glare turns deathly. "Because the cops are on the lookout for me and have people working for them. Which means I can't trust anyone," he snaps.

"Why are you here? What are you going to do with me?" I try to talk loud enough that Mr. Miller will be able to hear me if he answered, but not loud enough that it's obvious to Frank what I'm doing.

"I'm here to take care of what Tony should've done when he caught you in the gas station that night." He reaches into his suit jacket and I'm about to ask what he's going to do, but the words get stuck in my throat when he pulls out a gun and points it at me.

Forgetting my phone is in my hand I put my hands up in surrender, "Are you going to kill me?" I squeak out as my phone drops to the floor.

An evil grin spreads across his face. "Let's just call it revenge." He sees the phone on the floor and scowls. "You shouldn't have done that!" he growls. He stands up and walks over as he continues pointing the gun at me. He points the gun at the floor and shoots the phone. My eyes flick down to my now shattered phone, and it's then that I realize his gun has a silencer. My fear level begins to rise as it dawns that if he shoots me no one will hear the gunshot.

I glance up at the barrel of the gun and my panic escalates. It's about four to five feet away from me and he has it pointed at my head now. I don't know much about guns but it's some type of handgun. Maybe a Glock? I don't know but I have to get that gun away from him somehow. I'm not going down without a fight. I know if Mr. Miller has the police come and Frank hears the sirens he won't hesitate to pull the trigger.

I'm so focused on the gun that I don't see it coming. Frank takes his fist and swings it across the right side of my face. Pain shoots through my cheek and I gasp as I begin to taste blood. My hands immediately grab my face. My vision begins to get a little fuzzy and I can't see him clearly, but I can make out the outline of the barrel still pointing back at me. This is it. This is where he shoots me and gets what he came here for.

"Just for that I think I'll go after your friend Gavin when I'm done with you," he says menacingly. I freeze at Frank's words.

"Ah, yes. That got your attention, didn't it?" I can hear satisfaction in his voice.

"H-how do you know Gavin?" I knew that he was following me, but he shouldn't know Gavin's name, should he?

"He helped me out." I want to ask a million questions, but I know I'm running out of time. He could pull the trigger at any time.

I shake my head. "No, he wouldn't do that to me. You're lying!" I snap, trying to convince myself. Gavin wouldn't do that to me. He's always been there for me. He's one of my best friends. A burst of adrenaline hits me. I spot a lamp nearby and I don't hesitate. I step over to the right and grab the lamp with both hands. I use all my strength and swing the lamp at him. I'm not sure where I hit him but he stumbles a little and I hear the gun hit the floor. I look over and see the gun slide across the tile. Frank looks up at me and I freeze in place. If looks could kill I would already be dead.

He stands up and wipes the blood off his forehead. I must've hit him on the head with the lamp. "You're going to pay for that," he seethes. Both of us glance down at the gun, then back at each other. I go to dive for the gun and both of our fingers grab it. I use both hands to try to aim the barrel away from me and also get the gun from him. He's a lot stronger than me so I try to use my feet and kick him which makes him even angrier. Both our hands are wrapped around the gun again and we are fighting for it. I try to move off to the side but he shoves me back. Before I can aim the barrel away from me a shot fires off.

Startled by the sound, my hands let go of the gun and I fall back and hit the floor. It's then that I scream out in pain as my shoulder hits the floor. Agony shoots throughout my body and my shoulder feels like it's on fire. I look over at my left side and see blood soaking my shirt. I begin to feel lightheaded and my vision begins to get blurry.

I flinch when I hear another gunshot.

"Riley!" I hear footsteps approach me. I look over

and through the blur I see a silhouette kneel next to me. "Riley! I'm sorry!"

"Gavin?" I whisper, confused.

"Shh...You're going to be okay. I'm sorry! This wasn't supposed to happen, Riley!" I look into his eyes and see remorse. I'm confused why he is sorry and why he's here. As he continues to talk I only hear bits and pieces as I go in and out of consciousness. I don't understand what he is saying.

"I'm so sorry, Riley" is the last thing I remember hearing.

Then everything goes black.

CHAPTER 23

Jayce

Today is Thursday and I am officially done with finals. I'm so glad this semester is over. Tonight I'll be flying out to Virginia Beach and I'll be able to see Riley tomorrow morning. The last month and a half has gone by so slow. I've thought about going to see her ever since I got back, especially after hearing about the break-in, but I decided to wait until I finished this semester. I've been planning this since Daphne told me that she didn't want me to call her. Well, now that I'm done with school I'm going to spend the summer with her. I won't let her push me away again.

When I saw her on the beach that day, I thought I was imagining things. I had been thinking about her a lot at the time because her birthday was the last week of February and I knew she would've been turning twenty-one. I missed her like crazy. Then when I saw her lying there in the sand I was angry because I thought she just left me and didn't care about me at all. Of course now I know what happened and I hate that I wasn't there for her through all of that. Now she is going through all of it again and I'm still not there.

Well, that's all going to change because tomorrow I will be there. If this isn't over by the end of the summer I'm planning to transfer to a college in Virginia because I'm not leaving her this time. I love her. I've known that since we dated back in high school. I've dated other girls and none of them compare to her. She's the one that I want to spend the rest of my life with.

It's a little after one as I'm walking out of class and pull out my phone. I check and see I have four missed calls and voicemails from Daphne. That's odd. She knows I'm coming tomorrow. She wouldn't call me that many times unless....

I'm just about to call her when my phone rings. It's Daphne.

"Hey! I was..."

"Jayce! You need to get here now! It's Riley," she sobs. "She's been shot!"

I freeze and my heart drops. I have about a million questions but I can't get anything out. This can't be happening. She had people watching her to make sure something like this didn't happen. Right? How did this happen? They were supposed to protect her. Maybe I'll wake up tomorrow and everything will be fine.

"Jayce! Are you there? Did you hear what I said?" Daphne yells into the phone, snapping me out of it.

"Y-yeah. I'm here."

"Riley is at the hospital! You need to get here as soon as you can!"

I begin walking to my car faster. "What happened? Is she going to be okay?"

I hear her take in several deep breaths to calm herself down enough to talk. "I got home from class and there were a couple ambulances and a bunch of police cars parked outside our building. I tried walking up to our apartment but they wouldn't let me through. I asked what happened and they said that someone had been shot. I was about to ask who but then I saw them wheeling Riley out on a stretcher. She wasn't conscious, Jayce." She begins crying again.

I feel my own eyes begin to fill with tears. "Daphne..." I pause trying to keep myself from crying. "Is she going to be okay?"

"I don't know. They took her into surgery right away and we haven't heard anything. I'm here at the hospital with her parents and Gavin."

I'm not a jealous guy, but hearing he's there and I'm not doesn't sit right with me. "Why is Gavin there?" I try to hold in my irritation, but doubt I succeed.

"He's a friend, Jayce, but he's here because he might be the only reason she makes it." She takes a deep breath. "Just get on the first flight you can. Call me back and let me know the details."

"Okay. I'll call you back."

I hang up and am tempted to throw my phone. I'm angry. I should've been there, not Gavin. This is why I wanted to be there with her, so that I could protect her. The government was supposed to and they didn't. I can't lose her. Not now. I just got her back. I have a million questions about why Gavin showed up when everything happened but decide to push those aside for now and figure out how soon I can get there.

I get into my car and look up the airport's number. I call ticketing and try to get an earlier flight. After being on the phone with them for ten minutes I find out that they don't have any earlier flights than the one that I have, which makes me even angrier. I toss my phone onto the passenger seat and slam my hands on the steering wheel and let out a yell. I grip the steering wheel and lean my forehead on it. I finally give in and let the tears fall.

I don't know how much time passes but once I get myself calmed back down I pick up my phone off the passenger seat. I call Daphne and she answers on the third ring. "What did you find out?"

"There aren't any earlier flights. I'll still be flying out of Portland at ten o'clock tonight and won't be getting in to Norfolk until eight-forty tomorrow morning your time. I was hoping I would be able to get in today." I sigh, feeling defeated. "Have you heard anything yet?"

"Yeah, they finally came out and told us she was shot in the shoulder. They still have her in surgery right now to try to remove the bullet. So far they aren't sure how much damage was done but she is hanging in there. They said they would let us know once they know more." I want to hear for sure that she is going to be okay.

"Jayce, there's more." I hear movement and then she lowers her voice. "I was going to wait till you got here but I think you should know now. Just in case...something happens." She takes a deep breath. "Riley is..." She hesitates.

"Daphne, what is it?" I ask anxiously, needing to know.

"Riley is pregnant," she whispers. I sit there, shocked. I don't know what I was expecting Daphne to tell me but that wasn't it.

"Wha—," I'm so shocked I can't get the words out. I take a few deep breaths. "When did she find out?" How long has Riley known about this and why didn't she tell me? Is she happy about this? Or maybe she didn't even know.

"I don't know. She never said anything to me...we just found out. The doctor told us when he spoke to us."

"Is..." I'm afraid to know the answer but I need to know. "Is the baby okay?" I ask quietly.

"So far they think the baby is fine."

I release the breath I didn't realize I was holding. "Good. Well, keep me posted please. I won't be able to answer while I'm on the plane but just call and leave me a message if I don't answer."

"I will."

"All right, I'll talk to you later."

I hear her hang up and I lower the phone slowly. I can't believe I'm going to be a dad. I sit there and let all that sink in. Slowly I feel a smile spread across my face thinking about starting a family with Riley. Of course it's a lot sooner than expected, but that's okay. Now I just need to hope that they both pull through all this.

***

About four hours later I'm driving to my parents' house, and I'm just about there when my phone rings.

"Hey."

"Hey, I just wanted to call and let you know that Riley is out of surgery. The bullet fractured her shoulder and she lost quite a bit of blood. Right now she is in ICU being monitored closely."

"Is she going to be okay? When do they think she'll wake up?"

"They think she'll pull through this, but since she lost so much blood they want to monitor her closely. As far as when she'll wake up, they're not sure. She was unconscious when they brought her in. They said she could wake up once the anesthesia wears off or it could be longer."

"And the baby?" I ask quietly.

"They did another ultrasound and said the baby looks fine." She hesitates, and from the tone of her voice I know I'm not going to like what she has to say. "But Jayce, they said she could miscarry. With all the stress and shock of the situation it could cause her to lose it," Daphne tells me sadly.

I sigh. "I want to be there so bad right now. I hate being all the way across the country while Riley is laying in a hospital bed fighting for her life and the baby's."

"I know. Riley is a fighter though. She'll pull through this."

"I hope so. Have you been able to see her yet?"

"No, they won't let me go in. Her parents just went back to see her. Well, I need to get off here but I will call you if I hear anything more."

"Okay. Talk to you soon." I hang up as I pull into my parents' house.

The only person that knows I'm going to Virginia Beach is Ryan. Everyone else, including my parents, think I'm flying out to see some friends. It technically isn't a lie; I just didn't give them the details. Evan could see there was more that I wasn't telling him and tried to get me to tell him more, but I couldn't. I really wanted to tell Evan and Olivia that Riley was alive, but I told her I wouldn't tell anyone. I'm hoping that once this is over we'll be able to tell them. That reminds me, I completely forgot to ask Daphne if they ended up catching the guy. I'll have to ask her the next time I talk to her.

The next fifteen and a half hours seemed to drag on forever. Yes, I counted down the hours because I was so anxious to get to Virginia Beach and I couldn't get there fast enough. I hardly slept on the plane, and when I did it was only for a short time and then I would wake up again. All I could think about was Riley and our baby and if they were going to be okay.

When my flight touched down in Charlotte I checked my phone and had a voicemail from Daphne. She was just letting me know that Riley was moved out of ICU and was in a regular room now to recover. She still hasn't woken up yet, but the doctors seem to think that she'll pull through. That was a relief to hear.

When I called her back nothing had changed, but I was able to ask her if they ended up catching the guy, and I found out that Gavin shot him. So it looks like Riley will be safe now and we won't have to worry about him coming after her anymore. But hearing Gavin shot him and killed him brought all those questions from earlier back...Was he involved somehow? Why was he there at the time everything was going on? Was it just coincidence that he showed up? With a gun, no less?

I finally land in Norfolk at eight-forty in the morning and I can't get out of here fast enough. I get my luggage, and head over to pick up my rental car.

I pull into the hospital thirty minutes later, walk in and see Daphne waiting for me. As I approach she looks over and smiles sadly. "Hey. You made it."

"Yeah, finally," I sigh. "So, any changes?"

"No, still the same." She begins walking toward the elevators and I fall into step with her.

"Are they letting visitors in?" I hope they are now because I really want to go in and see her.

"Yeah, but they don't want you to stay for very long. I went in and saw her a little while ago." I glance over and see her eyes begin to fill with tears. "It was so hard to see her like that, Jayce. She's hooked up to some machines and she just looked so pale and...I don't know. Just not herself." Daphne sniffles. "I guess the guy must've punched her or something because her face is all bruised up." Hearing that not only did this guy shoot her but also hit her makes me angry. My hands begin to fist just thinking about it. I'm not a violent guy, but hearing that makes me want to hit something. If he wasn't gone I would probably track him down myself.

Daphne looks over at me. "I just wish I could've

gotten home sooner. I got there like fifteen minutes too late. I would've gotten there earlier, but I decided to make a quick stop at the store. I should've just went straight home." Tears begin to run down her face.

I grab her hand and pull her off to the side so people can get around us. I let go of her hand and look down at her. "Hey, you didn't know he was going to be there."

"Yeah, but I knew that she was in danger and he could show up at any time." She sniffles and wipes the tears off her cheeks.

"Daphne, stop blaming yourself. I did the same thing when you first told me. I was mad because I should've been here to protect her. I never should've left knowing that there was a chance this guy could come after her. But you know what? He would've found another time to try to get her. And hey..." I wait until she looks up at me, "She's still alive, and she's going to pull through this. She's not in ICU anymore so that's a good sign."

She nods and sighs, "You're right. She's alive and safe now, and that's what matters."

"Exactly. Now let's go see her."

Daphne leads me over to the waiting area first and I see Riley's parents. It's been almost three years since I've seen them. Riley's dad is sitting by his wife with his arm around her, holding her close. I walk over to them and they both stand and give me a hug, "How are you, Jayce?" Riley's mom asks.

"Better now that I'm here."

She pulls back and tries to smile. "Well, we're glad you're here. Maybe if she hears your voice she'll wake up." Her eyes glisten with unshed tears. I could ask them how they are doing but I already know the answer. I notice dark circles under their eyes, letting me know they haven't slept much. Riley's mom's eyes are swollen, showing that she has been crying. I can't even imagine this has been easy on them. This is what has haunted their dreams for the past few years, and now they are sitting in the hospital hoping their daughter will pull through and wake up soon.

"I don't know about that but it's worth a try. Right?" I say, trying to lighten the mood a little.

Riley's dad pats me on the back. "Here, I'll take you over to her room," he offers. I nod and follow him down the hall.

We stop outside her door. "I don't know if Daphne told you, but I just want to give you a heads up. I don't want you to be surprised when you go in. Her face is pretty bruised up."

Even though Daphne already told me just hearing it again infuriates me. Riley's dad must notice because he puts his hand on my shoulder. "I know, Jayce, I know. Just remember he can't hurt her anymore." I look over and nod. He turns around and walks back over to the visitor area.

I walk into the room and no one could've prepared me for what I saw. Riley looks so small and fragile lying in the bed. She has an IV hooked up to her arm and tubes coming from her nose that are hooked up to a machine. She has a black eye on her right side, and most of the right side of her face is bruised up and swollen. Her left arm is in an immobilizer holding her arm in place and she has bandages on her left shoulder where she was shot.

As I walk over to the bed and get closer I feel my eyes fill with tears. I pull the chair over next to the bed and sit down. I gently take her right hand and intertwine our fingers together, then bring her hand up and place a kiss on it. "Hey, Elle. I've missed you." I take a shaky breath. "I've missed you so much." Reaching up, I tuck a piece of hair behind her left ear and place my hand gently on her cheek. "I'm sorry I didn't go after you that night and fight harder for you. I should've been here for you, to protect you." I shake my head trying to hold the tears back. "I should've come sooner. But I'm here now and I'm not leaving you again. I love you." I feel the tears running down my cheeks. "I need you to wake up, Elle. You need to pull through this for us and for our baby." I lean up and carefully kiss her on the left cheek.

I sit back down in the chair. I look her over, hoping to see any sign of her waking up, but still nothing. "I can't lose you again, Elle," I whisper as I wipe the tears off my face.

CHAPTER 24

Riley

The fog slowly begins to clear from my head and I begin to stir a little. I go to lift my right hand but feel something has a hold on it. Panic overwhelms me; I feel like I'm trapped. I try to open my eyes to see what has me but wince in pain. Why does it hurt when I try to open my eyes? My breathing begins picking up and my breaths begin to come in shallow. I try to pull my hand away but the grip tightens. I try to move my left hand to pull my right hand free, but pain shoots out from my shoulder down my arm and I scream out in pain.

"Riley!" The grip on my right hand is released.

"Elle, its Jayce." I feel a hand on my left cheek. "You're safe. It's me."

I begin to relax at the sound of Jayce's voice and lean into his hand. "You're safe now, Elle." He rubs his thumb back and forth on my cheek.

I try to open my eyes again and flinch a little from the pain, so I decide to keep them closed. I go to say something but my throat is so raw that nothing comes out. What happened to me? Where am I?

"Here, take a drink of water." Someone, Jayce I

assume, places a straw up to my mouth and helps me take a drink. The cold water soothes my throat as it goes down. I take a couple more small sips, and he places the cup down.

He takes my right hand. "Can you open your eyes?"

I shake my head no. "Do you remember what happened?" he asks cautiously, and again I shake my head.

I hear him take a deep breath. "Frank was at your apartment and he shot you in the shoulder. He went to get away but Gavin killed him. He can't get you anymore." Relief floods my body as I hear that Frank is gone for good. "You're in the hospital. You had to have surgery to remove the bullet. You were unconscious for the first twenty-four hours, and then you have been waking up off and on for the last day and a half for short periods of time. When you did wake you were pretty out of it." He pulls my hand up and places a kiss on it. As he's talking the memories flood back. I remember going to my apartment and Frank being there. I tried to get the gun away from him and a shot was fired, and after that I don't remember. Hearing Gavin was involved confuses me. I feel like I'm missing something, something important. "We've all been waiting for you to come back to us." He reaches up and brushes my hair off my face. "I'm so glad you're okay." His voice comes out a little shaky, almost like he's trying to hold back tears.

Then all of sudden I remember. "The baby..." I whisper hoarsely. Is the baby okay? Does Jayce know? Jayce must feel me panicking because I feel him move up on the bed next to me. I feel him lean over my ear. "The baby is fine," he whispers, and I can hear the smile in his voice which tells me he isn't upset about the pregnancy. He places his hand on my stomach and I startle a little, not expecting it. I feel him lean toward me; he places a light kiss on my cheek and then I feel his absence as he pulls back.

I try to open my eyes again so I can see his expression. I flinch from the pain but eventually get my left eye open a little. Though it's harder to focus with one eye I can still see the joy and relief on Jayce's face. I wish I could've been the one to tell him about the baby. I wanted to be able to see his reaction and share the moment with him. I reach my right hand up and cradle his face. "I'm sorry," I whisper.

His brows furrow in confusion. "Sorry for what?"

I want to tell him everything I'm sorry for but my throat still feels raw, so instead I say, "Everything." And I am. I'm sorry for not being the one to tell him about the baby. I'm sorry for leaving him that night. And I'm sorry for pushing him away when I needed him the most. I feel my eyes begin to water.

"Hey, it's okay." He wipes the tears that have fallen down my face. "Everything is going to be okay now." He gently moves his arm around me and wraps his other arm around my waist as I lean into him.

After a few minutes I reach over for my water and Jayce hands it to me. I take a few more sips and hand it back to him. "Are you mad?" I ask, my voice coming out hoarse. He seemed happy about the baby when I asked about it before but I want to make sure he isn't upset about me being pregnant. I don't want him to feel like I tried to trap him or something.

He looks down at me. My eye still hurts so it's hard to really see, but I can tell he looks confused "Why would I be mad at you?" I look down at his hand that is still on my stomach. He follows my gaze and then gently lifts my chin up so I'm looking at him. "About the baby? No, I'm not mad. I was definitely surprised, but not mad."

I glance down at my stomach. "What are we going to do?" I ask quietly.

"We have time to figure out what we want to do, but I'm not letting you push me away again. I never should've let you push me away this last time." He reaches up and cradles the left side of my face and gives me a loving smile. "I love you and this baby." He grabs my hand and places both our hands on my stomach. I glance up and see he was waiting for me to look at him before he continues. "We're in this together. Okay?"

I feel tears stream down my face as I nod. I don't know how I ever let him go, but I know I won't push him away again. He lightly brushes the tears off my face so as not to hurt me and then leans down and places a kiss on my forehead. He pulls back and smiles. "Although I would love to continue having you all to myself, I should probably go let the nurse know you are awake. Also I know your parents and Daphne have been worried about you so they will all be happy to know you are awake." He gets up from the bed and begins heading toward the door.

"Jayce." I cringe a little because my voice is still so hoarse. He stops and turns around. "I love you."

His face lights up as he grins. "I love you too, Elle." Then he turns back around and walks out the door.

I'm just about to doze off when I hear people come into my room.

"Oh, honey! You're awake!" I hear my mom say as she rushes over to the bed. I slowly open my left eye, trying to avoid flinching in pain. She grabs my right hand and gently squeezes. "We were so worried about you," she says as tears stream down her face. "Are you in any pain? Do you need anything?"

Just as she asks a nurse comes in with a doctor following behind her. I look up and see Daphne, my dad and Jayce standing against the wall at the foot of the bed, and they all smile at me. My dad's eyes are watery but I can see the relief in his expression as he smiles at me. I really gave my parents a scare and of course this is something they were both worried about happening. I know it's not my fault but I still feel bad for putting them through all this.

"Hi, Riley. Glad to see you're awake and alert. I'm Dr. Goodrich, but you can call me Will." He smiles warmly at me. "I was going to discuss some things with you if you're up to it." He glances over at my dad, Jayce, Daphne, and then over at my mom. "Is it okay to discuss it in front of the other people in the room?"

I'm assuming that they already know pretty much what the doctor is going to tell me so I nod my head. He looks down at my chart then back up at me. "Okay. Do you remember how you got here?"

"No." I clear my throat a little bit. "But Jayce," I point over to him, "told me a little bit about what happened and the memories came back to me."

He nods. "That's good. Well, you suffered a bullet wound to the shoulder. You lost quite a bit of blood, but it wasn't enough that you needed a blood transfusion. We were able to remove the bullet, thankfully. The bullet did fracture your shoulder though so you will have to wear the immobilizer on your arm for a while to help keep your shoulder in place. How's your pain doing? Are you having any pain?" he asks with some concern.

"Yeah, actually my shoulder is starting to hurt. It also hurts when I try to open my eyes."

He nods and writes something down on my chart. "Okay, we'll get you some more pain medication soon."

Will looks back over at me. "Riley, were you aware that you are pregnant?"

"Yeah, I found out right before all this happened."

He leans forward and rests his elbows on his knees. "We did an ultrasound to check on the baby and so far everything seems fine." He hesitates and begins to look at me with sympathy. I already know that I'm not going to like what he says next. "I don't want to scare you, but I want to warn you that with everything that you have been through it puts the baby at risk," he says seriously.

I feel my eyes begin to fill with tears. "So what are you saying?" My voice comes out shaky as I try to hold in a sob.

"Sometimes too much stress on the baby can cause miscarriages. With being shot, losing a lot of blood, and having the surgery it may cause you to miscarry. I'm not saying it will, but I want to warn you that it could."

I feel the tears run down my cheek. "I-is there anything I can do?" I choke out.

"I need you to avoid stress and to relax. The baby is fine right now and everything looks good. So you need to take it easy, which you'll need to do with your shoulder anyway." He stands. "Debbie will be bringing you some medicine for your pain soon, and it will probably make you tired." He looks to both my parents and Jayce. "She'll need her rest so don't stay in here too much longer." He walks over to the door and turns back. "I'll be back tomorrow morning to see how you're doing. If you need anything just call for the nurse." Then he walks out of the room.

I begin to sob when the doctor leaves; pain shoots through my shoulder and makes me cry harder. My dad walks over and sits next to my mom on one side of my bed and Jayce goes over to the other. My dad grabs my hand. "It's going to be okay, sweetie. Everything is going to be okay."

I nod and try to calm myself down. I know he doesn't know if everything is going to be okay, but I have to hold on to that small amount of hope and believe that he's right. With everything that I've been through I don't know that I would be able to handle losing a baby too.

Once I'm calmed down my parents stay to visit for a few minutes before excusing themselves, saying something about me needing to rest and them needing to eat.

Daphne had been silent most of the time but once my parents leave she walks over to my bed. "Riley, I'm so glad you're okay." She places her hand on my arm. I look up and smile. I see her eyes begin to water.

I place my hand on hers. "Thanks. I'm sorry I gave you all such a scare."

She laughs lightly. "Just get some rest so you can get out of this place." She gently reaches her arms around to hug me and I hug her back with my uninjured arm. She pulls back and smiles. "I'll see you in the morning." Then she turns and walks out.

Once Daphne and my parents leave I look over at Jayce and notice him watching me. He seems a little on edge. "What was that?" I ask, referring to how quickly they all left.

"Nothing," he says innocently. I raise an eyebrow at him, letting him know I don't buy it.

He looks down at the floor and takes a deep breath. He seems nervous. Looking up, he locks eyes with me. He leans closer to me and gently holds my left hand. I look down as he intertwines our fingers, then glance up as he begins to speak. "Elle, I love you. I meant what I said the night you left Oregon almost three years ago. My love for you will never cease and it never has. Even when I thought I lost you forever I never stopped loving you." He gets down on one knee and my breath catches in my throat as I realize what he's about to do. "I know this isn't an ideal place to do this but I don't want to wait any longer. I don't want to spend any more time away from you. I want to spend the rest of my life with you. Will you marry me, Elle?"

I nod as tears run down my cheeks again, but this time they are tears of joy.

"Is that a yes?" he asks hesitantly. "And are those happy tears?" He brushes the drops off.

"Yes, I'll marry you." I smile through the tears. "And yes, they are happy tears." I laugh a little.

It's then that I notice that Jayce is holding an open black box. He lets go of my hand and takes a ring out. We lock eyes as he slowly slides the ring onto my left ring finger. "I can't wait for you to be my wife." He leans in and gives me a gentle kiss on my lips. He pulls back and we both look down at the ring and I gasp. "It's perfect, Jayce." The ring is a white gold with princess-cut past, present, and future diamonds. "I love it!" I look up into his eyes. "I love you."

He smiles down at me. "I love you too."

There's a knock on the door and we both look toward it. "Hi, Riley. I'm going to check your vitals and go ahead and give you your medicine." Debbie walks over to the other side of my bed and begins messing with the machines.

"Well, I'll let you get some rest." He leans down and kisses my forehead. "I'll see you soon." Jayce turns and walks out the room and the nurse begins taking my vitals. I feel the coldness seep through my veins as she gives me the pain medicine through my IV. Once she finishes she writes a few things down on my chart and then leaves the room.

Once she's gone I look down at my ring and can't help the grin that spreads across my face. I can't believe I'm going to be Jayce's wife and we're going to have a baby. Up until several months ago I thought I would never see Jayce again. I thought I would have to somehow find a way to move on without him, but now he's back in my life and we're going to be a family like I dreamed about for so long.

It's not long before my eyes become so heavy that

I can't keep them open anymore. I don't know if I imagine it, but right before I drift off to sleep I feel someone lightly brush their hand down my cheek. "Goodnight, Elle," is said so quietly that I'm not sure I really heard it.

CHAPTER 25

The next morning I wake up to nurses coming and going out of my room. Jayce somehow talked the nurses into letting him sleep in my room because when I awoke, he was asleep in the chair next to my bed. After breakfast the doctor came to check in with me and make sure my wounds were healing right.

Once the doctor left, Jayce and my parents decided to all go back to their house for showers and a fresh change of clothes. I could tell they were reluctant to go but I assured them I would be fine. They promised not to be gone long and told me they would bring me back some lunch, which I was excited about.

I'm watching some TV while I'm waiting when I hear a soft knock on the door. I figure it's a nurse so I continue watching the screen.

"Hey."

My body tenses as I look up and see Gavin hesitantly walk into my room. He meets my eyes and part of me begins to panic. I don't know how I feel about having him so close to me. I know he shot

Frank but I have so many questions for him and I don't know where to start. The last thing I remember was him saying he was sorry and me wondering what he was sorry about.

"What are you doing here?" My voice comes out shaky.

He looks me over before meeting my gaze again. "I'm glad to see you're doing better." He seems just as nervous as I am.

I decide to skip over the small talk and ask the question that I've been wondering about since Frank mentioned Gavin. "Were you working with Frank?" I ask slowly.

He breaks my stare and walks over to the chair next to my bed and sits. Looking down, he leans down and rests his elbows on his knees. "I'm sorry, Riley." I can hear the remorse in his voice. "I didn't know what to do."

"Answer the question, Gavin!" I snap.

"No, it wasn't like that. It's not what you think."

"Then explain it to me—all of it! You were one of my best friends. I trusted you!" I say, feeling betrayed.

He nods and meets my gaze head on. "I have a younger brother who has a gambling problem. Last summer he took a trip out to Vegas, and got himself into trouble. I found out that he owed Frank, who at the time was a bookie there, some money so I went to him to try to resolve it somehow. The minute I met Frank I knew that if he didn't get what he wanted my brother would be dead. Frank had just found out you were in Virginia Beach. He didn't tell me much. All I knew was he got your file somehow and it said you were here, but didn't give the exact location. He said if I came here and found you then he would forgive my brother's debt. So I accepted." He takes a deep breath. "I moved here and decided to enroll in classes for fall term, figuring it was the best place to start. I was relieved when the first day of class I saw you walk into my class. I didn't know for sure it was you, but I could see the resemblance. Anyway, I began getting to know you and I couldn't get myself to tell Frank that I had found you, so I pushed it off."

"Why?" I ask quietly. He found me. So why wouldn't he tell Frank?

"Because I knew Frank was after you for a reason. He wanted you dead. I held off telling him, trying to figure out a way to keep Frank satisfied and keep my brother safe."

"But why wouldn't you just tell him it was me? You could've been done with it all."

He sighs and looks down. "Because, Riley, I couldn't live with myself if something happened to you. I asked you out because I really liked you. That had nothing to do with the connection to Frank. When you ended it I knew that it wasn't going to work out. I knew once you found out everything that you would hate me so I settled for just being friends with you." I shift, feeling uncomfortable with where this conversation is going. After we broke up we never brought it up again. We just continued being friends like we never dated.

Gavin must notice the awkwardness because he continues. "Anyway, by spring semester Frank was impatient, so I finally told him you were in one of my classes. After that he wanted me to give him information on you such as your class schedule, friends, boyfriends, and anything else I could find. I didn't give him everything but I gave him enough to keep him off my back. Over Spring Break I saw my brother and Frank had begun making threats to him, saying I wasn't doing enough."

"That's why you seemed so different when you came back?" I whisper, more to myself then to him.

He must've heard me because he answers, "Yes. When I got back Frank told me if I didn't do what he said and give him what he wanted then he would kill you and your parents, my brother, and then me. So I gave him what he wanted. I also made sure to check in with you and my brother frequently." That explains why he seemed to be around a lot more than usual. I can't believe all this was going on. I never would've guessed that my messed up life intertwined with Gavin. I tried to keep that part of my life separate from my life in Virginia. That's why I pushed Jayce away. I didn't want anyone else involved but Gavin was involved all along. Part of me wants to be angry with him because he gave Frank information on me; he helped Frank find me. But how can I be mad at him when he was trying to protect his brother and in some ways me too? Would I do the same thing if I was in his situation?

"That day I took you to the clinic I wanted to tell you. Frank sent me a text to have me make sure you got to your apartment at a certain time. I knew what he was planning to do. I almost warned you, but I didn't have time if I didn't want Frank to get suspicious. So I decided to let you go and then I planned to show up before things got bad." His eyes begin to glisten with tears. "I didn't mean for anything to happen to you, Riley! I was trying to protect my brother and you at the same time. I got to your apartment just as Frank shot you and I didn't think twice. I pulled my gun out and shot him." He shakes his head as tears stream down his face. "I'm sorry, Riley. I don't know if you'll ever forgive me, but I never meant for you to get hurt. If you want me to turn myself in...I will."

I can see he's unsure how I'm going to respond. He's afraid. As I stare into his eyes I can't help but feel my eyes fill with tears. I can see how much regret he has for everything that has happened and I know he is telling the truth about it all.

"Gavin." I place my hand on his and wait for him

to meet my eyes. "I understand why you did what you did. I'm mad that you gave information about me to Frank. I trusted you as a friend and you betrayed me." I need him to know that I'm hurt by what he did. "But I understand why you did it. I'm so sorry that you were put in that situation. I don't want you to turn yourself in because to me you did what you had to do to keep your brother safe. But you also did your best to make sure that I was safe too. I want to thank you for that." I feel the tears run down my face. "Without you I might not be here."

Gavin looks at me, stunned by my response. After a few moments he finally asks, "So you don't hate me? I was the one that confirmed that you were here to Frank."

"I know that, but if you didn't confirm it then Frank would've sent someone else. Someone that wouldn't have thought twice about telling Frank. So no, I don't hate you." I smile to let him know I sincerely mean it. Maybe I'm being too forgiving but he was trying to protect his brother and he ended up saving my life too.

"That means a lot. Still friends then?"

I nod. "Still friends."

CHAPTER 26

10 weeks later

I walk over to the mirror, and look at the reflection. The girl staring back at me has grown up so much in the last ten weeks. The woman I see now has come a long way from the girl that was lying in the hospital bed.

Things have been busy non-stop since I got out of the hospital. I ended up being in there for another nine days after I woke up, so a total of twelve days. After I was released I began going to physical therapy appointments three times a week. I could've gone to the place that I worked at but I didn't want the people that I had worked with to ask questions. I ended up quitting the job altogether and moved out of my apartment. After everything that had happened there I couldn't go back. Daphne was a little bummed but she understood. She ended up moving into her brother's place and I moved in with my parents.

Once June came I decided I wanted to go somewhere else. I wanted a new start in another place that wouldn't remind me of everything that I had gone through that led up to me getting shot. I knew that Frank was gone but I still wanted away. I wasn't sleeping well between the nightmares and trying to sleep in a position that wouldn't hurt my shoulder. I would wake up in cold sweats, crying, and screaming. So I decided I needed out. Since Frank was dead I could've moved back to Oregon but I wanted a completely fresh start. I didn't want reminders of everything that I had gone through. I wanted to move somewhere warm, and of course by the ocean, so I decided on Galveston, Texas.

By mid-June Jayce and I were moved into a small two bedroom apartment. My parents decided to follow me to Texas too since there was nothing in Virginia Beach to keep them there, but they moved to Houston instead of Galveston. They wanted to be in a bigger city and were both able to get jobs there right away.

Jayce has stuck by me through all this. He pretty much hasn't left my side at all. He has helped me through my nightmares and everything that I've struggled with. I'm so thankful that he is back in my life. When we first looked into moving I wasn't sure if he would want to move so far away from his family and friends. But he said he was ready for a change, and ready for some warmer weather too. It worked out that he is going to be able to finish out his degree at Oregon State University. The courses he has left he is able to take online, so he will continue when fall semester begins. I missed my graduation since I was in the hospital but still received my diploma. We had a small get-together at my parents' house to celebrate me graduating. I'm not sure that I'll be getting a job anytime soon. I'm still healing from the bullet wound and going to physical therapy, but it's only once a week now. Plus in a few months things will be changing, and I will want to stay home anyway.

I reach up and place my hands on my belly and

smile. We did have a scare with the baby while I was in the hospital. I had started spotting a little but thankfully nothing came of it. Everything has been fine with the baby ever since.

I'm startled out of my thoughts when I hear the door open.

"Riles! You look gorgeous!" Daphne squeals as she walks over to me. I look in the mirror and can't help the grin that spreads across my face as I take in my overall appearance. My now honey blonde hair is styled half up and is in loose curls down my back with several curls that are left out to frame my face. I'm wearing more makeup than I usually do and it really brings out my facial features. Now for the finishing touch.

"Need help getting into your dress?" Daphne asks as if reading my mind.

I nod and walk over to grab my dress off the hanger. Today is the day I have been waiting a long time for. Jayce and I are getting married. In just a short time I will officially be Riley Lynn Cooper. We didn't have long to plan but we both decided that we wanted to get married before the baby came. To make the planning simple we decided to have a small wedding on the beach here in Galveston with just our parents, Evan, Ryan, Daphne, and Olivia.

"Are you almost ready? I think they are waiting for you," Olivia says as she walks into the room.

"Almost. I just need help getting into my dress." She smiles and she and Daphne begin helping me into my dress.

After I had been in the hospital for a week we got the okay that I could get in contact with people from Oregon. Jayce was finally able to tell his parents about me. They ended up flying out to see me, and were thrilled that I was alive and glad that I had pulled through everything that had happened. They weren't surprised that Jayce and I had gotten engaged because they always figured when we dated in high school that we would end up together.

When it was time to tell Evan and Olivia about what had happened I had Jayce talk to them first. I wasn't sure how they would respond and I didn't want to freak them out by calling them out of the blue when they thought I was dead. They both were stunned and couldn't believe it. We all cried and caught up on everything that has been going on over the last three years. They were going to fly out to see me but decided to wait until the wedding.

Olivia and I have talked pretty much every day and sometimes we video chat. Things are still a little awkward for us because this whole time she thought I was dead, so we're adjusting to the idea of me being here and being able to talk to each other.

Once I'm in my dress I walk over to the mirror. When choosing my wedding dress I wanted something that would hide my bullet wound, but still something that I could stand to wear in the heat. I look in the mirror and smile. The dress is a white empire-style floor length gown with lace sheer cap sleeves. The lace goes over just far enough to cover my wound.

Daphne and Olivia come over and stand by me in the mirror. "You look beautiful!" they both say in unison and we all laugh.

"You both look beautiful too." I look over both of them. They are both wearing knee-length light pink dresses. The dresses are the same empire-style look as my wedding dress with the high waistline. We are all wearing matching light pink T-strap sandals. Daphne is my maid of honor and Olivia is my bridesmaid. I turn to give them both a hug. "Thank you guys for everything. I'm so glad you both were able to come. I don't know that I could've gotten this wedding planned in such a short time without your help." I begin to feel my eyes water. "I'm so emotional now," I laugh as I wipe under my eyes.

I walk over and grab our bouquets, and hand Daphne and Olivia theirs.

"So will you tell us what the baby names are that you have picked?" Olivia asks excitedly.

"Nope, sorry. Jayce and I aren't telling anyone the name until after the wedding," I smile.

For our wedding colors we chose light blue and light pink. Daphne and Olivia are wearing pink dresses and Evan and Ryan are wearing tan dress pants and light blue button up dress shirts. We had our ultrasound a couple weeks ago but declined to find out the gender. The tech placed the results in a sealed envelope, and when we ordered our wedding cake we gave them the envelope. We wanted today to not only be about Jayce and me, but also our baby. So today when we cut our wedding cake we will find out if we are having a boy or a girl. Once we know we are going to announce the name we have picked out.

Daphne walks over and places my veil in my hair and smiles. "All set!"

"We better go before the guys send a search party for us," Daphne laughs.

Once we walk out of the room my dad is waiting for me. When he sees me approach his eyes light up as he smiles at me. "My little girl is growing up! I can't believe it." His eyes begin to water. "You look beautiful, honey." He walks over and gently gives me a hug, being careful of my shoulder. I still have to wear the arm sling most of the time to keep my shoulder in place, but I decided I would be okay through the wedding.

"Dad, you're going to make me cry." He pulls back and holds out his arm for me to take and I do. He beams down at me. "Are you ready?"

I nod. We follow Daphne and Olivia down to the back door that leads out to the beach. We rented a vacation house right on the beach so we would have a place to get ready for the wedding ahead of time.

As we get to the door I look out just as Jayce has made his way up to where he stands next to the pastor. I take in the scene and can't help but smile. The wedding really did turn out perfect. There is an archway that is covered in white fabric, and the white is held off to the sides with light blue and light pink fabric. Down the aisle there are pink and blue flower petals that line the way to the arch. On each side of the aisle there are two white folding chairs for each of our parents. Jayce's parents are already both seated, and so is my mom.

I move off to the side as Evan and Ryan come over to the back door. "You ladies ready?" Ryan asks.

"Yep," we reply. I look over at Ryan and see that he is watching Daphne, but she ignores him and looks down at her flowers, pretending to fix them.

"Great, I'll let them know," Evan says as he steps outside the door. He gives the pastor and Jayce the signal that we're ready and the music begins to play through the speakers that have been set up.

Evan holds his arm out for Daphne. She hooks her arm with his and they head out toward Jayce. Then Olivia turns to me. "I'm so happy for you, Riley. You guys deserve this." She smiles as she walks over and gives me a quick hug. She pulls back and hooks her arm with Ryan and they begin to walk toward the others.

"Are you nervous?" my dad asks.

"Nope, I'm ready." I grin up at him. We turn and begin walking out. Once we step outside the song switches over to the "Wedding March". Our parents stand and everyone turns toward me as we begin our walk to Jayce.

I look up and lock eyes with the man I love. My heart skips a beat when I see his face light up as he grins back at me. His eyes shine with so much love and happiness. He looks so handsome standing there in his tan dress pants and white button up shirt. As I get closer I notice his eyes glistening with unshed tears. I begin to feel my own eyes fill the closer I get to him. This is really happening. I'm finally marrying the boy I always dreamed of marrying back in high school. I never thought I would see him again. I never thought I would be able to make things right between us. And I never thought that we would get married after I left Oregon, but Daphne was right. This was our second chance, and I'm so thankful that we got it.

My dad stops us a few feet in front of Jayce. I turn toward him and he pulls me into a hug. "I'm so proud of you sweetheart. I love you," he whispers before he pulls back.

I look up and smile through my tears. "I love you too, Dad." He gently takes my hand and walks me the few steps to Jayce and hands me over to him before going to his seat.

I gaze up at Jayce and can't help but grin. He reaches up and cups my face. "You look amazing, Elle." He tenderly wipes the tears off my face, then takes my hand and intertwines our fingers together. We walk up to the pastor together and then turn to face each other as he begins the ceremony.

The pastor begins and reads a couple verses from the Bible. After he explains the importance of our vows, we join hands and the pastor nods for Jayce to go ahead.

"Riley." I look up into his dark chocolate colored eyes. "I've told you before that what we have is special. It's rare and unique. I knew it from the moment I first saw you. When I saw you three years after you left Oregon, on the other side of the country, it only proved what I already knew. Everything that we have gone through...the chances of it happening were so slim that it's almost impossible. Yet here we are. We were given the second chance that most people only hope for." My eyes fill with tears again and I feel a drop slip down my cheek. Jayce pulls me closer so that we're a few inches apart. "But we got it, Elle. I promise you I won't take that second chance for granted." He reaches up and cradles my face in his hands. "I love you, Elle. That has never changed and it never will. I promise." He again wipes the tears that are running down my face and smiles. "And I promise to love this baby and all of our future children too. I promise to be the best husband and father that I can be."

All I want to do is wrap my arms around this wonderful man standing in front of me and never let go. But instead I take a few deep breaths and get my emotions under control. I reach up and take his hands in mine again then look into his eyes and hope he can see the love that I have for him. "Jayce, you are my best friend. You have helped me through some of the toughest times of my life and you have also been there for some of the greatest moments of my life, and I'm so thankful for that." I close my eyes and take a deep breath, trying to hold in my tears. I open them and look back at Jayce. "I promise to be faithful, to be supportive, and to never take you for granted. I promise I will love you and our family through sunshine and storms forever more." And I can't hold back the tears anymore as I think back to the text Jayce had sent me about not worrying about the storms, and the response I'd sent back. I see that he recognizes it too as his eyes begin to water.

After the vows the pastor asks for the rings and we exchange them. Once we finish the pastor looks from Jayce over to me and grins, "I now pronounce you husband and wife." He tells Jayce, "You may now kiss your bride."

Jayce doesn't hesitate as he places his hands on each side of my face, and I wrap my arms around his waist. He leans down and gives me the sweetest kiss.

We pull away grinning and turn to our parents and friends as they all clap and cheer.

After they all come up to congratulate us and give us hugs Jayce turns to everyone. "Who's ready to find out the baby gender? Follow us!" He grabs my hand and we begin to walk over to a table that is set off to the side.

Jayce and I stand behind the table and he picks up the knife. "Inside this cake will reveal the gender of the baby. Once we know the gender we will announce the name that Riley and I picked out." He smiles and looks over at me. "Are you ready, Mrs. Cooper?" He winks and I can't help but melt hearing him call me Mrs. Cooper for the first time. Grinning, I look up at him and nod.

He hands me the knife and covers my hand with his. We lower the knife into the cake and cut a small square. Jayce hands me the server and I scoop it out and place it on the plate. We both look down and my eyes begin to water with tears of joy. We look back up at each other, grinning.

"Aaron Matthew Cooper," Jayce says as I hold up the blue-tinted cake for everyone to see.

"It's a boy!" we announce in unison.

ABOUT THE AUTHOR

J.R. Brown is a young mother and wife who lives in the Midwest. Several years ago, she took up a love for reading. The more she read, the more she began to come up with her own ideas. It wasn't until recently that she took those ideas and created her own stories. She currently enjoys writing young adult romance novels.

For more information about J.R. Brown, visit her website:
www.jrbrownbooks.com